Succubus
LOST

From the Files of the Otherworlder Enforcement Agency

TIFFANY ALLEE

Previously released on Entangled's Ever After imprint – May 2012

Entangled Publishing, LLC
2614 South Timberline Road
Suite 109
Fort Collins, CO 80525
Visit our website at www.entangledpublishing.com.

Covet is an imprint of Entangled Publishing, LLC.

Edited by Kerry Vail
Cover design by Curtis Svehlak
Cover art by Depositphotos

Manufactured in the United States of America

First Edition May 2012

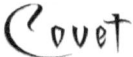

To my husband, for being a much bigger softie than he likes to admit.

Chapter One

The smell hit me first. Not decay, like I'd expected after being called to the site of a homicide, but cremains and trash.

Spotlights and flashlights lit the darkened alley, casting eerie shadows onto the asphalt and against the brick of the surrounding buildings. It was enough to make a person imagine threats that didn't exist, monsters hiding in the shadows. Surreal.

The alleyway behind La Maison wasn't exactly as nice as the lobby of the chic Chicago hotel, and the night air was cooling quickly. I glanced longingly toward the back door of the building and clutched my blazer a little tighter around me, wishing I'd worn pants instead of a skirt for once. Inside the hotel door lay the kitchen, and past that was one of the nicest lounge bars in the city, as well as a first-rate restaurant. Putting on my cop face — a slightly knowing smile that my friend Mac called "smug with a touch of haughty" — I followed Astrid into the Dumpster-filled alley where a metal trash can seemed to be the source of the ashy scent wafting down the street.

"I'm Astrid Holmes, and this is Marisol Whitman." Astrid flashed her badge at a police officer and a man in a crime scene investigator's jacket. I did the same. This was her case, so I'd follow her lead. "What do we got?" she asked, her voice almost too official.

The CSI spoke first. "Freak squad, huh? Looks like a body, burned."

Neither Astrid nor I so much as blinked at his rude greeting. It wasn't the first time we'd been called freaks, and it almost certainly wouldn't be the last.

At our lack of reactions, the CSI continued. "We won't know for sure until we get the cremated remains back to the lab, but we've got bits of teeth, some melted fillings, and small pieces of bone." Again the middle-aged man in the CSI jacket paused as if waiting for a dramatic response. The Chicago wind kicked up, and the ash smell grew even more pungent. Something living had definitely burned here.

"We've got guys going through this Dumpster again, and a couple of teams checking out the Dumpsters nearby," the uniform said, giving the other man a bored glance. "Just in case some evidence was stuffed into one of them."

"Who found the victim?" Astrid asked.

"Kitchen manager of the bakery." He nodded to a building on the opposite side of the alley from the hotel. "Says he saw someone heading outta here fast, around four thirty this morning, but he didn't get a good look at him. Big guy, he said."

"No wonder he didn't see much out here," I muttered. Sure, there was a lot of light with our equipment in the area, but otherwise the whole shadowy space would only have been lit by a single standing streetlamp. I squinted at the light.

"Yeah, especially since it happened in the middle of the night—well, technically early this morning. The man who chased the guy called us, but since he couldn't say for sure what the guy was doing, a unit didn't get out here until ten this morning. It took us a while to figure out the ashes were human, then we didn't know whether it was one of yours or not. Lieutenant said to call in your sensitive, though. That she'd be able to tell."

Astrid's attention had slipped away from our conversation, and her gaze was affixed on the metal trash barrel less than twenty feet away. As a sensitive—a human naturally gifted with the ability to feel magic and energy—she was probably itching to check out the remains.

"Why don't you go have a look-see," I suggested. "I'll finish up here."

Astrid's eyes widened and she nodded, then hurried away. The girl really needed to work on her cop face.

I gleaned a few more bits of information from the uniform, who was more than willing to talk the case with an attractive succubus. Yes, they'd questioned the manager. No, he didn't seem like he was hiding anything. No, they hadn't found anything else to suggest this was a murder scene, but their techs were scouring the area for blood as we spoke.

Unfortunately, my succubus powers weren't very helpful with gaining more information from a fellow cop who was already being forthright. Although my unconscious powers were likely loosening his tongue, between my questions he just jabbered incessantly about things like the weather and my eyes. Poor thing probably thought he was flirting. Luckily for me and my job security, unconscious powers were not illegal to use—they were just a part of an otherworlder. That's why lots of police departments and government agencies loved to use vampire interrogators. The aura of fear vamps carried was an effective tool to get people to cooperate. A sexy aura didn't always work as well as fear.

Astrid caught my eye as I interrogated the cop. Facing us, she stood over the metal barrel, hands open, palms down over the trash container. She didn't seem to be touching anything but was as close as humanly possible without violating any evidence-handling rules.

She frowned and then walked around the barrel, turning so her back faced our small group. I waved the officer off and walked toward her. Careful to keep my heels quiet against the asphalt, I gave her a wide berth and made my way around to stand a few feet in front of her, but off to the side.

As I took in her expression, I smiled. Her brows were drawn together as she concentrated. Her mouth formed a sour expression, like she sucked on a lemon. When her features were taken together, her expression was truly dramatic and altogether silly.

Suddenly, she let out a small sigh and her face relaxed. She opened her eyes and gave me a level look. "Please quit staring at me. It makes me paranoid about how I look when I need to be concentrating."

My cheeks heated, I muttered an apology, and then turned my attention to the asphalt around me.

"Actually, if you wouldn't mind…" Astrid's voice was hesitant.

I raised an eyebrow at her. "What? I'm not watching, I swear."

"No, it's just…it's harder to get a read if an OW is nearby. Muddles things up a bit."

Oh. No wonder. Astrid could feel the energies of any otherworlders around her. If I lingered, my succubus energy could drown out or jumble any traces she might pick up from the remains. "Got it," I said, making myself scarce. I went to look for the uniform and CSI who'd first talked to us. Couldn't hurt to make sure we'd gotten every bit of information from them possible.

Interrogation was what I was good at, after all.

Light from the window pressed against my eyelids, and I threw an arm over my face. Damn curtains. I'd been more than a little drunk when Astrid had dropped me off the night before. What had I done? Opened them?

Astrid convinced me to get a drink after our sweep of the crime scene left us with little to go on until we got some lab work back. Then we lamented over our normally laughable cases, and having someone on the less-dangerous end of the otherworlder scale to talk to made me feel like I wasn't alone in my general assignment of crappy cases. A fact that didn't make me feel a whole lot better that I was usually relegated to interrogating suspects in the safety of the station. At least Astrid caught good cases because of her vampire partner sometimes, although she was lucky they let her out of the office with Claude out of town.

I tottered to the bathroom and stepped into the shower,

yelping as the cold water hit me. Slowly, my brain unfuzzied and I was able to dress with a modicum of stability and care. I carefully applied makeup and styled my long blond hair into a loose chignon. Satisfied with my appearance, I wandered down to the kitchen, grabbed my teakettle from the stove, and filled it.

It had been a long time since I'd allowed myself to get more than just tipsy, even with people I trusted.

The source of the stress I'd needed to drink off was none other than my boss. Lieutenant Vasquez's face flashed in my mind and I pushed down the anger that followed. I was a good cop, even if he thought I was nothing more than a bit of fluff, a conwoman who could get men to confess with her false charm. And I was good at training new detectives, even if Vasquez never gave my partners and me any particularly challenging cases.

I reached into the cupboard next to the stove and pulled out a teabag, then grabbed a cup from another cabinet. It wasn't entirely Vasquez's fault. I knew that. New detectives rarely got the toughest cases, especially when they were partnered with a succubus. As far as otherworlders went, succubi weren't the toughest—or anywhere near the most fearsome—species. Not that we couldn't be stronger than the average human, but that required feeding. And in order to stay sane, that would necessitate, at the very least, a long-term partner.

I hadn't had even a boyfriend in years. Not since before Elaine was attacked.

The teakettle whistled, and I suppressed a sigh of pure self-pity. The clock read ten, and some terribly important shoes awaited Elaine at the mall. Shoes she needed my credit card to purchase.

"Elaine!" I yelled at the open loft area that led to Elaine's bedroom. "Time to get up. Shopping was your idea."

I grabbed the newspaper off the front step, wandered back to the kitchen, and opened it. As I listened for the sound of the upstairs shower, I scanned the articles. Getting Elaine up and around had never been an issue until she'd started college, and she rarely stayed out obscenely late, but her new ability to sleep well past what the rest of the world considered morning was another small adjustment.

When silence still permeated the house after I'd made it to the comics, I poured myself another cup of tea and hiked up the stairs. Elaine's shift from shut-in to social butterfly had gone clear past normal kid and into the realm of super student. She managed to hold a very aggressive academic schedule and do very well at it. But how did she expect to add a part-time job onto her load when she couldn't even get herself up? Not that she'd gotten around to doing more than talking about looking for a job.

I paused. She never slept with her door open, but I heard nothing from the bathroom to my left, and that door stood a few inches ajar as well. Hands shaking, I pushed her bedroom door open and my stomach twisted at the sight of her bed. Corners tucked just so, made in the hotel fashion that I used when helping her put new bedding on.

I touched the bed. My head grew light and I took a deep breath. She hadn't slept here last night.

I raced down the stairs to the house phone and hit the voice-mail button. No messages. I grabbed my cell phone and touched the screen. No texts. No voice mails. Nothing.

I swallowed around the cold rock growing in my throat.

With trembling hands, I hit her name on my cell phone screen. She was fine. It had gotten late while she was studying so she'd stayed with Wendy. Or maybe they'd gone to a party and she was passed out on the floor somewhere. I'd kill her when I found her.

The phone rang a few times, and then a computerized voice came onto the line, informing me that the person I had called was unavailable and could I please leave a message.

Eyes burning, I took a deep breath. "Hey, it's me." I was going for light and airy, but even to my own ears I sounded like I was on the edge of tears. "Where are you? Call me as soon as you get this." I hit end and concentrated on my breathing. I had to stay calm. She was fine, and calling her friends while hysterical wasn't going to make her happy with me. But the possibility that something was really wrong was too frightening. I couldn't be worried about embarrassing her.

I hit Wendy's number and concentrated on the sound of the ringer in my ear. Four rings, six, finally Wendy's voice came onto the line. My stomach lurched.

Voice mail. Personalized with a message from Wendy, but voice mail all the same.

"Wendy, it's Marisol. Tell Elaine to call me ASAP," I snapped.

She was fine. She had to be.

Chapter Two

I flung the door open and strode into Vasquez's office. Ignoring the two uniforms already seated in front of his old metal desk, I asked, "Where are we at?"

Vasquez nodded at the uniforms. "Grady and Parks are headed out to canvass the library." He gave them each a picture of Elaine. Her DMV photo had been blown up, and the portrait looked fuzzy and unreal. The officers got up from their seats.

"Her hair is different." I swallowed hard, trying to rid my voice of its strangled tone. "I don't have any photos of the new cut, but it's shorter than in that one. Shoulder length around her face and shorter in the back." My hand shook as I waved it around my face. At their blank looks, I added, "Like Missy, the new receptionist. But blond."

Their wide eyes narrowed in understanding, and they nodded in unison before heading out the door.

I leaned against one of the guest chairs and met

Vasquez's hard gaze. "What else have you started? Did you get the missing person report filed?"

"It hasn't been twenty-four hours. Hell, Marisol, you don't even know if she's been gone twelve."

I struggled to keep my voice even. "You know that every second she's gone makes it more likely we won't find her."

His mouth was drawn in a hard line, but worry creased his brows. "I know. But she's a college student. How do you know she didn't just meet some guy—"

"She wouldn't do that! She…" My nails dug into the vinyl lining the back of the chair. Telling Vasquez about her past wouldn't help me. He'd just assume the worst of her, more so than he already did. A boy in her high school had decided that Elaine was fair game because she was a succubus. He'd attacked her, and lost his life for it. Elaine was still more than a little fearful of men showing any interest in her, but Vasquez might see things differently. Might decide that because she'd killed before, she was some sort of criminal.

Vasquez got up from his desk and walked slowly around it. He reached for his office door and I blinked at our audience. Every eye in the station was directed at us. I swallowed a sob, and Vasquez slammed the door shut.

"Look, Whitman, I know you're worried—"

"Please! Jesus Christ, Vasquez! What if she were your sister, or your daughter?"

Vasquez frowned and considered it. I met his gaze with my own and refused to look away. I pushed my worry and fear and dread into my expression, hoping he would understand. Finally, he looked down.

"All right. We'll send out some more officers. But we can't put everyone on this."

I sat down heavily. "What about Claude? Is he back in town?" The vampire could help. He had great senses, sure, but even more than that, he had resources in the vampire community. Ones he might be willing to tap for a colleague. Claude had never shown me anything but respect, and his good-hearted nature had shown through his actions more times than I could recall. He'd help.

"Desmarais is out of town for at least three more days, on personal business. He specifically asked not to be bothered, and he told me he'd be unreachable anyway. I'm not tracking him down to help find your sister—who in all likelihood is playing hooky."

"Fine. I'll take Astrid." I pushed up from the desk.

"No. I'll send out a few more officers, but I'm not taking Holmes off a murder investigation." He raised an eyebrow. "Where am I sending the officers?"

I stopped, halfway between sitting and standing. Where should they go? One set of uniforms was already en route to the library where Elaine had supposedly been studying.

"The campus," I said around the lump in my throat. "See if anyone outside the library saw anything. And there's a pizza place not far from there they liked to go to after studying." I rubbed my temple, remembering the time I'd picked Elaine up from the restaurant. She'd looked so happy. Finally.

"Name?" Vasquez asked. I looked up at him. "The pizza place?"

"Oh. It's, um…" My mind went blank and I forced back tears. What the hell was the name of the pizza place?

"Never mind," Vasquez said. "We'll find it. Go talk to her friends."

I nodded, unable to trust my voice.

Wendy Larson didn't answer her door, so I moved on to the other friend of Elaine's I'd met, Teresa Robertson. Teresa's address put her in a downtown apartment building, and I parked directly in front, ignoring the NO PARKING signs guarding the curb. I trotted up the steps and scanned the list of names on the front of the building, then pressed firmly against the one that read ROBERTSON.

Unlike Wendy and Elaine, Teresa was a normal. The fact that she chose to spend most of her time with a couple of otherworlders surprised me, but she was a nice girl. And she didn't seem to mind that Elaine was a succubus or that Wendy was a siren. Part of a generation where OWs had always been a fact of life, Teresa was a bit more open to the idea of otherworlder friends than older normals were.

"Yeah?" The young woman's voice was staticky over the line, but I recognized Teresa's deep tones.

"Teresa, it's Marisol Whitman, Elaine's sister."

There was a pause, and then she said, "Elaine isn't here."

I took a deep breath. It had been a reach to think I might find her at Teresa's, but I'd still hoped. "Can I come up and talk to you? It's important."

"Yeah, sure." The door buzzed and I yanked it open and stepped inside. What passed for a lobby in Teresa's building was small, and covered in brown carpet that carried obvious stains. The small mailboxes that had been incorporated into one wall were the only things that broke up the room. A stairwell rose at the end of the narrow room, with a hallway next to it leading to the first-floor apartments.

I walked up the stairs to the third level and knocked on the fourth door on the left. Apartment 308.

Teresa opened the door almost instantly. Eyes wide, she stepped back and let me in. The small apartment was a studio style. The bed sat in one corner of the large room and a couch sat against the other wall. A small television was sitting on a dresser next to the bed, right across from the couch. A tiny kitchen was off to one side, with a bathroom across from it. The apartment was small but tidy. No sign any crazy party had happened there lately, and no sign of Elaine.

"Is everything okay?" Teresa asked.

Teresa looked like a deer in headlights, and I suddenly realized that I'd only met her once, when Elaine brought her to the house for a study session. I pasted on a smile and did my best to make it soothing instead of forced.

"I hope so. When was the last time you saw Elaine and Wendy?"

"Last night at the library. We headed out together, but they went to the south parking lot and I took the L."

"Elaine didn't take the L?"

"No, I think she was planning on it, but—"

"So she left with Wendy? Did they talk about going anywhere else before they headed home?"

"No, it sounded like they were going right home." Her eyes were still wide, like any moment she expected me to pull my gun.

"I'm sorry, Teresa. I'm not trying to scare you, but I haven't seen Elaine since yesterday. She didn't come home last night."

Teresa grasped her hands together and tugged her

fingers nervously. "She didn't come home? That's not like her."

I nodded, doing my best not to yell that I was well aware the behavior was very unlike my sister.

"They didn't say they were going anywhere else. I'm sorry. I just assumed they went home."

"Why didn't you ride with them?" Wendy's apartment was less than a mile from Teresa's.

Teresa shrugged. "I was going to my boyfriend's. He lives up north."

I paced in Teresa's small room. From the end of the bed to the end of the living room. Back and forth. Teresa watched me, nervously chewing on the inside of her cheek.

Halting in midstride, I pivoted to face her. "Nothing unusual happened at all yesterday? I need to know everything. Start at the beginning, from when you met them at the library. Every detail you remember. Every. Thing."

Teresa took a deep breath and began her story.

I pulled into the parking lot, taking one-and-a-half spaces, then strode into the station. Vasquez's door was closed. I paused in front of it. Barging into his office not once, but twice in one day? I steeled myself. I didn't have time for knocking.

I swung open the door and stepped inside. Vasquez sat across from a handsome man I didn't recognize.

"Thanks for knocking," Vasquez said, but his voice lacked anger.

"No one has seen Elaine or her friend since last night.

I'm going to pull contact information for Wendy—the friend she was with. But we need to file a missing person's report on Elaine now, Vasquez."

The lieutenant's eye twitched at my lack of proper address, but he didn't call me out for it. I guessed that having a missing sister helped my latitude with him. "Already done, Marisol." He gestured to the man across from him. "This is Agent Valerio Costa. He's from the OWEA. I've already briefed him on your sister's case."

The Otherworlder Enforcement Agency was a federal investigative force similar to the FBI, but they mainly investigated crimes that involved otherworlder victims and criminals. Why would an OWEA agent be interested in Elaine?

I nodded at Costa. Even sitting, he looked tall and deceptively slender because of his height. I could make out the muscles under his dark gray button-up shirt. He wasn't built like a meathead, but he definitely visited the gym regularly. His nose was hawk-like and a touch imperfect, like he'd broken it a few times. Black hair topped his head and waved around his face, softening his otherwise sharp features, and I had the sudden desire to brush a lock of hair away from his face with my fingertips. Dark brown eyes met mine—not angry, but hard and closed-off.

Costa reached out and I met his hand with my own. He shook it, his fingers firm and almost cold against mine. I frowned and examined him more closely.

"Vampire?" The question was rude, but propriety was the least of my worries. I needed to know who I was dealing with. He didn't have the slight paleness that vampires were known for, but then he may have fed recently. No fear emanated from him, but that didn't disqualify the vampire angle altogether, since some vampires exuded more fear than others.

A grimace touched Costa's features, gone so quickly I wasn't even certain I saw it. "Salamander."

"Ah." Salamanders were essentially a type of elemental. They could control fire and were resistant to its effects. I didn't know any personally, but they weren't the rarest of otherworlders, and most were only slightly more powerful than a match.

"Agent Costa is investigating the disappearance of succubi around the country."

My heart skipped, and I dropped Costa's hand as if the cold had suddenly been replaced with fire.

"Tell me." My voice was firm and void of the emotion that boiled just below the surface.

"Nearly twenty succubi have disappeared from various locations around the country over the last two years. Most young, under thirty." Costa's voice was deep and smooth, with a hint of an Italian accent.

"None...recovered?" I asked, fearing his response.

"They are still considered missing, not presumed deceased."

I dragged out the chair next to Costa's and sat down heavily. "Why do you think they're still alive?"

"We've picked up rumors of a man who is selling succubi to the highest bidders." He paused and took a deep breath, eyes on mine as if assessing my ability to take whatever news he was about to give me. I met his stare with a hard expression that seemed to reassure him that I could take it, but he glanced at the lieutenant and waited for his slight nod before continuing. "It seems he's selling them as sex slaves."

My stomach dropped and the room spun. I gripped the arms of my chair and tried to grasp my thoughts. God. With everything Elaine had already been through, it just wasn't fair. Couldn't be real. "That doesn't make any sense. Succubi can kill with their powers. It can be suppressed with drugs or magic, but then they wouldn't be any more interesting than normal human women. Why target succubi?"

"We're not sure. The bit of information we've been able to glean is unreliable, and it varies depending on who we talk to. The one consistent rumor is that they're still alive. And that's what you should focus on."

I opened my mouth to tell him not to tell me what to focus on, but then snapped it shut. My strength was in my ability to deal with people, even bossy, know-it-all OWEA people. I'd get more info from him playing nice than playing hardball. "All right. What else do we know? I'll need some specifics."

"I'll get you files on the victims and the case summary I've put together so far. We need to figure out where they took your sister and how. This is the quickest a disappearance has been reported, so we might be able to get them while they're in the area."

"Wait—when exactly did you get into town?" I asked through gritted teeth. "Did you know there was a danger and not warn us?"

Vasquez turned a suspicious glare to Costa, but the OWEA agent didn't look the slightest bit uncomfortable under our scrutiny.

"I got into town last night. There was another kidnapping here several months ago, and then two weeks ago a succubus disappeared in Phoenix. The one here took a while to get reported, since she was estranged from her family. My partner is in Phoenix right now. I didn't expect them to hit the same city more than once in such close succession." He met my gaze. "I got lucky."

I flew from my seat and Costa grabbed my wrists to protect himself from the blows I was trying to level at his face.

"Get off him, Marisol!" Vasquez barked.

"I'm sorry," Costa said. "That was…a poor choice of words."

Poor choice of words. Yeah, sure. I yanked my wrists out of his cool hands and sat back in my chair.

"I really am sorry," he murmured.

I looked up at him. His mask had fallen just enough for me to see that he meant his words. Or that he wanted me to think he did, anyway. I gave him a short nod, not trusting myself to speak.

Costa cleared his throat. "I would like your help on the case, if you don't mind. My partner is in Phoenix for a few more days, at least. I could use another investigator."

"Of course!"

"Now wait just a damn minute," Vasquez said. "This is personal. No way am I putting her on this. Her judgment is impaired."

"My judgment is fine," I snapped, pushing myself up from the chair to tower over the seated lieutenant.

"Normally I'd agree with you, Lieutenant," Costa said, voice back to smooth and confident. "But Whitman is the only succubus you have at the detective level in your squad, and I think a succubus could be helpful in this case. Perhaps you will allow me to consult with her, if not involve her directly in the investigation?"

Vasquez looked like he wanted to argue, but finally he said, "Fine. Though if I think your investigation is in any way harming my officer, I'll have your badge, Costa." He turned his gaze to me. "And don't forget you're not off the hook with helping Astrid. Claude will be back in a couple of days, but she may need some backup in the meantime. If nothing else, the murder investigation should keep you out of trouble."

Chapter Three

"Where are we going first?" Costa asked after Vasquez's office door shut safely behind us.

I blinked at him.

"Come on," he said, one eyebrow raised. "I'm not an idiot. I didn't really believe your lieutenant's orders were going to faze you."

I cleared my throat. "I need to look up some info on Elaine's friend Wendy. She's a siren, and I haven't been able to track her down. She was the last person to see Elaine as far as I've been able to tell. I'm afraid something has happened to her, too."

Costa nodded and gestured for me to lead the way. The man was cool under pressure. Most people—otherworlder or no—would have pressed for more info or shown more emotion when I mentioned Wendy's species. Sirens were relatively rare and almost always stayed away from humans as much as possible. Their abilities were very powerful, and that made normals and otherworlders very suspicious of them—more so than succubi, even, which was quite an accomplishment.

I walked to my desk, unusually self-conscious with Costa behind me, and far too aware of him. When we reached my computer, I sat and logged into the national police database.

Costa placed his hands on the back of my chair, and I was careful not to lean back and touch him. I needed to stay focused on Elaine. He leaned forward and his scent swirled around me. Aftershave and something spicy that could only be him. I closed my eyes for a second before I snapped them back open. *Priorities much?*

"So tell me what you've learned so far."

I pursed my lips. "I talked to her friend Teresa. Normal, twenty years old. She spent the afternoon and early evening with Elaine and Wendy at the library. Nothing unusual. Studying, girl-talk."

"Nothing at all unusual? Are you sure?" Costa cut in.

"Yes, I'm sure. I know how to question a witness." Costa didn't comment, so I continued. "At the end of the night, Teresa left for the train station. Elaine and Wendy headed the opposite direction, toward the lot where Wendy's car was parked." I typed Wendy's name and address into the police database.

"Did you get any other info?"

"No. There wasn't any other info to get." I suppressed a sigh when the screen came up with little more information than what I already had. I'd figured Wendy wouldn't have a police record, but I'd hoped she might. It would have made our jobs just a hair easier. "We'll need to go to the college to get contact info for Wendy's family. She's not in the system.

Given the situation, hopefully they won't give us a hard time about a warrant."

"Full name?" Costa asked.

"Wendy Larson."

"Do you mind?"

I slid out of the chair so he could sit. He pulled up the national database and logged in. I frowned at his list of options, which were far more extensive than my own.

"Are you going to read over my shoulder?" he asked.

"That was the plan."

He stiffened but continued his search. A few quick clicks later, he ended on a page with a Skokie address.

The wheels squeaked as he rolled the chair out from under the desk. "Let's go meet the parents."

Wendy Larson's parents lived in one of the wealthier suburbs just north of Chicago. With access to the Red Line, one of the trains leading directly to various locations in the city, the neighborhood was desirable for people who worked in the city, but who also wanted the slower pace and free space that could only be found outside of the high-rises.

Costa parked in front of the quaint white home. With its shutters and large front porch, it would have fit in a small town in the southern part of the country more so than a Chicago suburb, and I wondered if her parents actually used the old wooden swing that hung on the porch.

I knocked on the door, trying to ignore the sensation of Valerio Costa's body standing so close behind mine. The coolness that had clung to his hands when they touched me at the station seemed to cling to his whole body, and I shivered.

"Are you cold?" he murmured.

"I'm fine, thank you."

Saved from his response by the door opening, I almost sighed in relief at the sight of the woman behind the door. Dark brown hair tucked into a neat bun at the base of her neck, she looked so like Wendy that I would have guessed them to be sisters. But Wendy didn't have a sister, so the tall woman had to be her mother.

"Annette Larson?" I asked

A quizzical look on her face, she nodded. "Yes, I'm Annette."

"My name is Marisol Whitman, and I'm a detective with the Chicago Police Department. This is Agent Costa. We need to talk to you about your daughter."

Her polite smile faltered. "What? Is everything all right? Has there been an accident?"

"We hope everything is okay. And we don't know that anything has happened to Wendy, but we need to speak with her, Mrs. Larson."

She waved us into the foyer but didn't invite us farther. "What is this all about?"

"When was the last time you spoke to your daughter?"

"I talked to Wendy last week; she was fine."

"Is your husband home?" I shot a quick glance to Costa. He was the lead investigator on this, so why was he letting me do all the talking?

"No. Frank is out of town."

"We'd like to speak with him, as well."

"He's quite unreachable. And he hasn't talked Wendy.

They don't keep in touch." She crossed her arms, and her face hardened. "What is this about?"

"Wendy hasn't been seen since last night when she left the library with another young woman who has been reported missing."

"Excuse me? Last night? Do you have reason to believe that something has happened?" Her voice was tight, as if she spoke through gritted teeth.

"No…it's just…" I struggled with how to explain.

"The other young woman, for reasons we can't divulge, is unlikely to have spent the night away from home if not coerced," Costa said.

Mrs. Larson let out a high-pitched laugh. "Oh my goodness, how silly. You come to my home and scare me. Make me think my daughter may be in danger or hurt. All because some overprotective parents can't believe their daughter stayed out overnight?"

"That's n-not—" I stumbled over my words, trying to figure out how to explain in a way that wouldn't sound stupid.

Her amusement dropped as suddenly as it appeared. "Get out. Get out of my house." She stomped a foot and pointed at the front door. "I don't need you people coming in, worrying us. Take your prejudices elsewhere."

I looked at Costa, desperate for him to say something, do something, but instead he reached out and gripped my elbow, hand still cool against my skin, even through my jacket. Lightly, he tugged me toward the door.

I searched my mind for a response, any kind of response to make her take us seriously, but it was as if all my training had never happened, all of my experience was null and void.

As we stepped through the doorway, Mrs. Larson barely waited for us to clear the frame before slamming the door behind us.

"So what was that, exactly?" I finally asked as we waited in line for a table at The Grill House.

Costa glanced at me, and though I tried to keep the anger boiling in my stomach off my face, I wasn't entirely certain I was successful.

"She hasn't talked to her daughter in more than a week. I'd be surprised if she spoke with her any more often than the occasional birthday or holiday. We weren't going to get any information out of her."

I tapped my foot and stared at his calm face. "How do you know that? We barely got anything out of the woman."

"I've been doing this a long time."

I crossed my arms and raised my eyebrows at him. "Been doing this a long time? Can you vague that up a bit more for me?"

A grin touched his lips, and the small expression transformed his face from merely handsome to dangerous. "All right, if you're going to demand all my secrets. She was hazy as to when she'd last talked to her daughter. Not like she was hiding something, but like she wasn't sure or didn't want to admit how long it had been. She was practically bathed in guilt. Something has happened in that family to alienate their daughter."

"Humph," I said. "Let me guess—given enough time you could have figured out what that was without her saying."

His grin broke into a full smile, and I found myself smiling in return. "I could probably make a few good guesses now."

I made a whoop-de-do gesture with my hand and turned to smile at the hostess. I considered telling Costa that I'd gotten the same impressions he had from Mrs. Larson, but decided against it. Being underestimated was something I was really good at, and it might be my only advantage with the OWEA agent. I'd check Wendy's phone records, but I imagined it had been quite a long time since she'd talked to her parents.

"It's probably because she's in college," I muttered.

"Excuse me?"

I frowned. I hadn't meant to speak aloud. "Wendy's mom. I'll bet she doesn't talk to Wendy much because her daughter's in college."

His brows drew together like he wanted to ask more, but the hostess interrupted us. "Detective," she said, "we have a table ready for you and your friend." She turned her smile to Costa and he nodded at her, his face once again covered by the serious mask that seemed to be his default expression to the world.

She seated us in a booth and the waitress who moved in to take our order was one I knew by sight, if not by name. Bright blue hair spiked on top of her head to form something that reminded me of blue fire. A professional smile was affixed to her face.

"Hi there, I'm Lisa. Can I get you guys something to drink?"

"Water," Costa said.

"Lemon?"

"No, thank you."

She turned her attention to me. "And for you?"

"Hot tea, please." I gave her my practiced smile before looking back to Costa as she hurried away from the table.

"So what you were saying before, about the sirens. I know that they're supposed to be a bit xenophobic, but do you really think the woman—even though she's a siren—would quit talking to her daughter over something like college?"

"Yes," I said simply. "They aren't just xenophobic. They believe strongly in not mixing in with normals or even nonsiren otherworlders. It's self-preservation, and you can hardly blame them for it. Their powers are unique and powerful. People tend to fear them. How much do you know about sirens?"

"I know that they have the power of suggestion."

That was one way to put it. "If you hear a siren sing, you do what they want. Period. For a time after you hear the song. The amount of time depends on how powerful she is—but it's generally thought to be short. Only a few minutes if she doesn't sing you under again."

"So it's similar to a succubus thrall," he said, bitterness lacing his tone.

I grimaced. "No. Not really. What sirens do takes away all willpower for the time you're influenced, without cost to them. But, once it's over, it's over. They can't control a person or make them forget. That's why the few sirens who have used their song on victims have almost always been caught and punished."

"Unlike a succubus, who can ruin your whole life if you let her, without cost." The bitterness in his tone turned to anger.

I stared at him. "Actually, the succubus takes a big risk using her powers, too, you know. The emotional connection built between a succubus and her mate is lasting, and it affects her just as much as it does him."

He shook his head, as if denying the truth in my words, and then leaned back in the booth and put his hands behind his head. "Surprised that doesn't hurt after a while."

"Pardon?"

"Keeping that fake smile on your face all the time." No amused expression touched his face, and he looked genuinely quizzical.

"It's not fake."

"Really? Your kid sister is kidnapped and you have it in you to smile at strangers?"

I took a deep breath and closed my eyes for a moment. When I opened them, he was frowning. "I'm able to do what I have to do, act how I have to act, in order to stay on this investigation, no matter how much I want to drop my smiling cop face." I waved, gesturing around the restaurant. "Do I feel like breaking down in this restaurant, crying for my sister?"

"Do you?"

I opened my mouth to give him an even bigger piece of my mind, but Lisa approached with our drinks, so I nodded gratefully at her instead.

She pulled out her notepad. "Ready to order?"

"Give us a minute, would you?" Costa asked.

"Sure thing." She gave him a big smile and sauntered off. The man was far too attractive for his own good. Too bad he was so unfriendly.

"So, do you? Feel like breaking down?" Costa asked.

I took a sip of my tea and studied the strangely cold man across from me. He was handsome and sexy in a way that made my succubus side shriek to get his attention, but there was something off about him. "Do you have any family, Agent Costa?"

"Yes." His voice held no emotion.

"Then you should understand how I feel right now. You should understand the lengths I will go to, the compartmentalizing I will do, in order to save my sister. Besides." I gave him a big smile. "Acting is something I'm very good at."

"Oh, I don't doubt that." Costa leaned forward, placing his elbows on the table, and I couldn't look away from his dark eyes. He opened his mouth, and a small flash of emotion crossed his face—so quickly I couldn't identify it—then he snapped his lips shut. He shook his head and leaned back in the booth.

"Are you guys ready to order yet?" Lisa rematerialized next to me and I barely covered a little jump by reaching for my teacup.

My stomach rolled at the idea of food, but I forced myself to say, "Salad with chicken, please."

Costa grimaced at my order. "Southwest burger. Fries."

The waitress jotted down our order and slipped her pen into a pocket at the front of her smock.

Silence overtook us for a few brief moments after the waitress left. Costa's eyes burned into me, far more intensely than they should. I was tempted to meet his stare, if only to pinpoint the exact shade of his eyes. Surely they were just deep brown? They seemed so dark that they verged on black, but that had to be because of the lighting.

I cleared my throat with a light cough and kept my gaze

firmly affixed to my tea. "Tell me more about the other cases."

He inhaled deeply, and then let the air out in a *whoosh*. "That could take a long time."

I gave him a sharp look. "Summarize."

"Fine. Over the last couple of years, succubi have been disappearing from around the country. A connection between the disappearances wasn't made until recently."

"Why did it take so long?"

He shrugged. "They took place in large cities, usually no more than one or two per city. Succubi aren't rare...as you know. And the women weren't connected by anything but species—aside from being young and attractive. Of course, that's hardly a rare trait in succubi. Not much else connects them."

I tapped my fingers on the table. "So they all just disappeared without a trace. Any sign of any other connected OW disappearances, like Wendy's?"

"No, and we haven't connected any other disappearances to those of the succubi." He grimaced. "But that doesn't mean it hasn't happened. We should look into other oh-dub disappearances around the same timeframe in the same cities as the succubi who have gone missing." He pulled out a small notepad and scribbled something on it.

We sat in awkward silence, me pretending to check important e-mails on my cell phone, and Costa going through his notes, until Lisa dropped off our food.

"So none of them have turned up dead. Do you have any evidence that..." I paused. I didn't really want to know, but I had to. "Do you have any evidence that they are still alive—other than not finding any bodies?"

He hesitated. "A psychic. One of the best in the OWEA. She's touched several of the victims' personal items. Some haven't been in contact with the items for long enough, so she couldn't get anything clear off of them. But some of the more recent ones she's gotten images...I don't know. Whatever they get. She says they're alive."

"Touched them, huh? A psychometrist, then?" Psychometrists were one of the rarer forms of psychics, able to glean information from touching objects. I hadn't seen many used in cases; Chicago PD didn't have one on the squad and Vasquez wasn't too keen on them. They were useless with cases most of the time unless we had a murder weapon. And even then, their visions weren't always clear. And unclear evidence didn't make it to court.

"One with a bit of clairvoyance. My partner."

My mouth dropped and I snapped it shut before Costa could comment on my surprise. Clairvoyants were especially rare. They didn't just get information about the past and present of objects and their owners, they occasionally got visions of likely events in the future. A psychometrist with a touch of clairvoyance was a stunning combination.

The fact that he had proof beyond a lack of bodies settled in, and a weight moved from my chest. She was alive, then. Almost definitely alive. That meant I could save her. I could get her back. I could bring my sister home.

Worry flitted in the back of my mind. What if she wasn't the same? What if they did something to break her? No. She was strong. She'd been through a lot. And she wasn't that easy to break. I could still see her face the night she'd killed that boy. She'd stumbled in from the cool night, hair a mess of twigs and leaves and dirt. Mascara ran down her cheeks, carried by long, hopeless tears. And her eyes—they carried a look of haunted horror that broke something in me.

Ever since, I'd struggled to help her get her life back. It had taken a few years—no wonder, considering the psychic damage on top of the mental and physical—but she'd recovered. She'd regained her confidence. She'd started living her life again.

I was going to get her back.

"Hello. You with me?" Costa waved a hand at my face.

"Just thinking. What else have you learned?"

"Not much. The kidnappers take one or two per city, usually a week or so apart. They move onto the next city after a month or two, same M.O. We've found no physical evidence, no unusual circumstances leading to their disappearances. They've all just seemed to be heading to work or to school." He took a drink of his water, and I did my best not to tap my nails on the table. "Like I said, the only thing they've had in common other than their species is their age."

"Look, just get me the summary. And the files. Okay?" I took a couple of bites of my salad and then grabbed my jacket. "We need to get moving."

He nodded and took a couple of huge bites of his burger, and half the sandwich disappeared. I tossed some cash on the table while he struggled to chew and keep his mouth closed.

We made it to the front door before he'd swallowed enough of the burger to mumble, "Where are we going?"

"The library."

Chapter Four

The library, with its imposing dark brick facade, towered over us as we approached the main entrance. Intimidating, it stole my breath and made my stomach clench, and I wondered if it had made Elaine feel the same way.

"You all right?" Costa paused at the entrance.

No, I'm far from all right. "I'm fine." I pushed past him and went through the door.

Washed-out neutral colors coated the floors and walls, covering the fabrics and hard surfaces of the room. Students lounged on couches with books, or at tables—leaning across to consult their friends on math problems or their love lives. A few sat in front of library computers. Several stood in line, waiting for a librarian to check out their books, fidgeting and antsy, probably wishing they were anywhere but the library.

I made my way to the checkout desk, cutting in front of the next girl in line. She made a rude noise and turned to gesture to her friends, who were already checked out and waiting for her near the front entrance.

The librarian gave me a disapproving look when I stepped up to the counter, but her annoyance faded when I
flashed my badge.

"I'm Detective Marisol Whitman. This is Agent Costa."
I nodded toward him. He stood behind me, a wall between
me and the students. Almost as if he watched my back—
protected me. Something inside my chest softened at the
thought. "We need to speak with whoever is in charge of
security."

The gray-haired woman nodded and picked up a phone
from the counter. She hissed in what was no doubt her
library voice, "Yes, there are some police officers here. Yes.
I'll send them over."

I tapped my fingernails on the counter as she finished
up her conversation and caught Costa watching my nervous
twitch. Frowning, I drew my hand back and crossed my arms
over my chest.

"Well, then," the librarian announced, voice losing all
semblance of its library tone. "One building over. The head
of security is the corner office, last door on the left." She gestured toward what I could only guess was the other building
and watched us expectantly. I had no doubt she'd be gossip-
ing about us and the disappearance to every student who
ventured into her line the moment we were out of earshot.

The head of security's office proved as easy to find as the
librarian promised, and JONATHAN DONOVAN was etched in
bold black letters, dark against the light shining behind the
glass. I stopped in front of the door and tugged my hair loose
from the carefully styled chignon and fluffed it around my
face. Then I took off my blazer. With the jacket on, my skirt

suit looked perfectly appropriate. But removing the blazer revealed an undershirt that looked positively sinful. Thin sleeves did nothing to cover my shoulders, and the just-shy-of-plunging neckline revealed quite a bit of cleavage. The soft fabric looked thinner than it actually was, and the ensemble clung to my body.

For the purposes of interrogation, the showy blouse was my armor. My disguise.

"Nice shirt," Costa said dryly. Then he leaned in from behind me, arm brushing my shoulder, and rapped on the door. He was too close again; I could feel him, smell his spicy scent. I resisted the urge to lean back, just a couple of inches, to touch his hard chest.

The door opened to reveal a balding man. Wearing my three-inch work heels, I stood only a hairbreadth under six feet tall. The top of Mr. Donovan's shiny head barely reached my chin. Eyes peered out at me through thick glasses, which he pushed up as he examined me. My worry over how Costa would feel about my outfit faded at the look of blatant interest on Donovan's face.

"I've already spoken with the police this morning. They just left, in fact," he said briskly. "I'm afraid I don't have all day to talk to you people."

"You're going to have to free more time in your schedule, Mr. Donovan." Costa's voice came out rough behind me.

Mr. Donovan frowned but gestured for us to come inside. A small bit of sweat beaded on his brow, and I wondered how such a thin man could be hot in this chilly office. The room resembled a closet more than a proper office, and the space felt too small for the three of us. I glanced at Costa. He didn't look uncomfortable. Maybe it was just me.

"We're sorry to inconvenience you, Mr. Donovan. I'm sure that you have very important duties to attend to," I said smoothly, pasting my professional yet slightly flirty smile on my face. Despite Costa's heavy-handedness, I was confident that honey would, in this case, net us far more information than his rougher methods.

Donovan relaxed and gave me a small smile in return. "I don't mind, Detective…?"

"Oh, I'm sorry! You can call me Marisol."

His smile grew then dimmed slightly as he shot Costa a less friendly glance.

"This is Agent Costa from the OWEA," I explained, keeping my attention fully on the head of security. I tossed my hair behind my shoulder and Donovan's eyes fixed back on me. Good. "Anyway, did you know either of the missing girls?"

"I'm sorry, but I don't have much contact with the students." He sat straighter in his chair. "I'm quite busy."

"Of course. Can you find out who was working in the library yesterday afternoon?" I pulled a small notebook and pen out of my inside jacket pocket.

"Well, you met Barbara Fuller. She was working the checkout desk yesterday, too. We didn't have any other full-time staff during the afternoon and evening, just students hired through the work assistance program. I gave their names to the other officers."

"Do you routinely keep track of who is working the library, Mr. Donovan?" I asked.

A nervous laugh escaped him. "The officers who were here earlier had me call down and check."

I suppressed a grimace. We might well be just repeating

what other cops had already done, but I couldn't risk not going through the steps, just in case they'd missed something. "If you wouldn't mind, it would really help me out to get the student staff's names as well."

"Of course."

"We'd also like to speak with Ms. Fuller," I added.

He frowned. "Well, she's off in a couple of hours. She said she didn't have anyone to cover the desk until then."

"Could you figure something out so we could speak to her? Maybe a student who works in the library could cover for her? I'd *really* appreciate it." My perfected expression eased into something work appropriate, but it was close to being inappropriate.

Red splotches crept up Donovan's thin neck. "If it would help, of course I'll see if there's someone here who could cover for her."

He picked up the phone, but before he could dial, I asked, "What about security cameras?"

"I'm sorry, but we don't have cameras in the library. No budget for it." He shrugged and Costa and I got up from our chairs.

I gave the man a small wave as we exited the office and suppressed a smile as he stumbled over his words into the phone.

I put my blazer back on when the cool fall air surrounded me, and I walked in front of Costa to the sidewalk that led down into the library. As I approached the door, he grabbed my arm, just under my shoulder, and pulled me to a stop. His grip wasn't rough, but it was firm.

"What?" I asked, angling my shoulder away from him so he'd release me.

He let go, and his arm grazed my breast as his hand fell away. I took in a quick breath and glared at him.

"What the hell was that?" His voice was cold, but not void of emotion.

"Excuse me?" My mouth dropped open and I snapped it shut, ignored the way my pulse skipped faster under his gaze.

"Do you really think flirting while on the job is appropriate?" Anger coated his tone, giving it a hard edge. "I'd think you could feed your desires on your own time."

Heat flared in my chest and rushed up to my face. "What the hell are you talking about?"

"Come on, any idiot could tell that you were coming on to that little weasel."

"An *idiot* might think that, yes," I hissed. I spun around and marched through the library doors. What the hell? Did he really think I was desperate enough for a lay that I'd flirt on the job, the day after my sister was kidnapped, with a guy as unattractive as Donovan? Asshole. He probably didn't know any way to get information out of people that didn't involve strong-arming.

Swallowing my anger and ignoring Costa trailing behind me, I stomped back to the checkout desk. Barbara Fuller gave me a small wave. As Costa moved into her view, her eyes widened and then she snapped them back to the next person in line, obviously unnerved by whatever expression I'd put on the OWEA agent's face. She helped the student, and then moved away from her post as a young woman came to replace her.

I tapped my foot and motioned toward Ms. Fuller. She walked up to us, hesitant, and I plastered on my pleasant smile.

"Thank you for taking the time to speak with us, Ms. Fuller," I said.

"Of course," she said, and tension faded from her stance as she examined me. She uncrossed her arms and pointed to a small meeting room next to the front desk she'd just vacated. "We can speak in there, if you would like some privacy."

"That would be wonderful. Thank you." I kept the smile firmly affixed to my face.

"So," she said as she shut the door behind us, "what can I help you with? I'm afraid I don't know much."

"You said the police spoke with you earlier? Can you tell us what you told them?" I asked.

She nodded and her eyes lit up with excitement. I gritted my teeth and pushed down the flare of anger I felt at her reaction. This was probably the most dramatic situation the librarian had seen in her life.

A laminate table with several chairs surrounding it filled the small room. Ms. Fuller sat facing the door and I sat across from her. Costa eyed the door and dragged a chair to one side. The placement allowed him to keep the door in his periphery while watching Ms. Fuller at the same time.

"Well, as I told the other officers, I know all of the girls by their pictures. I didn't know any of them by name except Wendy, though. They were all very nice. Quiet, you know? They didn't cause me any trouble when they studied here." She smoothed invisible wrinkles out of her blouse.

"Were you able to catch any bits of their conversation lately?" I asked. "Even something from several days ago could be relevant."

"I'm sorry, I just don't pay that close of attention. And like I said, the girls were quiet."

"Did you see anyone else talking with them?" Costa asked.

She thought about that for a moment. "Not that I remember, no. I'm sure other students talked to them—they seemed very popular—but I didn't notice anyone in particular."

"They seemed popular? Why do you say that?" I asked.

She waved a hand in the air. "Oh, you know. They were just that popular type. Pretty. Giggly. Popular."

I opened my mouth to ask her exactly what she meant by that description. My sister was smart—just because she was pretty that didn't give the woman the right to assume she was an airhead—but Costa gave me a warning glance and spoke before I could.

"Can you recall any of the students who spoke to them more often than others? Any students who spoke to them this week?"

I stood up from the table, startling Ms. Fuller. I'd had about enough of her assumptions and Costa's attitude. If he wanted to ask all the questions, then I'd let him. We weren't going to get any information from this woman anyway. We were just fodder for her gossip. "I'm going to look around. Can you finish up here?" I smiled at Costa, knowing that for once my go-to expression looked forced, if not outright angry. I turned and left without waiting for his reply.

The chilly air cut through my jacket as I made my way out to the parking lot. I walked the path Teresa said Wendy and Elaine headed toward the last time she'd seen them. I pulled on my gloves and took in my surroundings. The area was bustling this time of day, but Wendy and Elaine left the library late. Nine o'clock. There would still be people around then, wouldn't there? This was a college campus, after all.

I could remember my college years vividly. There hadn't been a lot of money, so I'd settled for a close commuter school that offered me a small scholarship. It was enough to get me into the police academy. And it had given me time. Time to grow into my succubus powers. Time to learn to control them and keep them compartmentalized within me until I needed them. Time to start to grow into the adult I would become.

I'd wanted something better for Elaine. Because she hadn't had the luxury of becoming a succubus slowly. Because she didn't get to feel safe. She had to live at home, but she did get to go to this beautiful campus.

A campus that now looked cloaked in danger.

I walked the couple of blocks to the parking lot, keeping my eyes on the area around me. There were too many places a person could have hid along the path. Behind a tree, crouched next to a trashcan, standing in plain sight—it wasn't like that would look out of place on a college campus.

The same gray haze that seemed to cover everything else also coated the parking lot. Rain wasn't falling yet—not really—but a slow drizzle coated the air and the dark fall sky was oppressive. Cars packed the large area to the brim, and like most college campus parking lots, not a single space remained free.

Well lit and recently painted, the parking lot didn't look like the kind of place that women just went missing from. Then again, people disappeared from perfectly normal-looking places every day. But two women disappearing together was highly unusual.

A lone officer—one who'd been assigned to the case while I was in the office with Vasquez—stood by a car not far from where I'd entered. When I approached he nodded to me.

"Is this Wendy's car?" I asked.

"Yes, ma'am. Just waiting on a warrant."

I gave the small Ford a once-over, careful to avoid touching it. I didn't see anything unusual. The girls probably hadn't even made it to the car. My gut clenched at the thought, and the small amount of hope I'd carried that we'd find a quick link to their kidnapper slipped away. The vehicle wouldn't contain any evidence to help us find Elaine and Wendy, and identifying where exactly they had been taken would be difficult. Never mind finding any evidence that could actually be linked conclusively.

I studied the parking lot carefully. The lights—something about them drew my attention, but they were tall enough that I had difficulty making out exactly what was off about them. I strode to the closest one and looked up, then blinked at the object adjacent to the light dumbly, as hope blossomed in my chest.

Security cameras.

Chapter Five

"What do you mean, the data's gone?" My voice rose to a shriek that even my half-banshee friend Mac would have been proud of.

"I'm sorry," Donovan said. "I don't know what could have happened to the footage. Like I told the other officers, nothing like this has ever happened before." Sweat trickled down the sides of his face.

"And you didn't think to mention this to us earlier?" I asked. Donovan's gaze darted to his hands. Of course he hadn't mentioned the cameras and lost footage. The little weasel hadn't wanted to get yelled at.

"Isn't there some sort of backup system?" Costa asked. He touched my shoulder and I shrugged him off.

"Not really," the head of security said. "The system records everything onto a hard drive. It's eventually deleted, but only when it's downloaded and archived. But everything from the last week was deleted—that was everything on the drive—and it doesn't seem to have been archived. We've never had a problem like this before. I—"

"Well, you've got a problem now, buddy. Maybe you should go find someone who actually knows how to do his job." I held my facade in place with the thinnest of emotional threads.

Red-faced, the head of security stuttered that he would get someone on the phone from the security company who sold the school the system, and he disappeared into his office.

I paced the hallway and Costa, eyes hooded, leaned against the wall and crossed his arms. After a few minutes, I calmed down enough to stop pacing. Donovan approached, his arms and head pulled close to his body like a dog expecting to be hit, and Costa pushed away from the wall.

"I'm sorry, Detective, but it'll be a while before I have any information for you." He glanced around. "I could call you," he said, hopeful.

I opened my mouth to tell him that I would wait, but my cell phone rang before I could get the words out. I pulled it out of my pocket and looked at the number. Astrid.

I touched my phone's screen. "Hello?" I took my wallet out. Astrid's voice came over the line as I handed the head of security my card.

"Hey, Marisol. It's Astrid. I'm so sorry about your sister."

"Thanks," I whispered. I cleared my throat and shoved my wallet back into my jacket. "We'll find her, so there's nothing to be sorry about."

"I hate to ask this, but are you busy right now?" she asked, voice tentative. "I need your help with something, if you have time."

I covered the phone's microphone. "Can you wait here

for the footage? I have something I need to do on that other case."

Costa nodded curtly, and I lifted the phone back to my ear. "What do you need?"

"So tell me again why you need me to talk to the witch?" I asked. Astrid and I stood in front of Natalie Leigh's high-rise office building, and its shiny walls glittered even when surrounded by dark gray skies.

Astrid frowned. "I don't need you, exactly. I just don't really care for witches, okay?"

I raised an eyebrow but didn't press her. Covenant witches were a secretive lot, and I couldn't blame her for not liking them. Only the vampires compared to the Covenant for political power in the otherworlder arena. Witches and vampires were powerful, and more plentiful than most other species. And more importantly, they were two species that were drawn to power. They sought it, fought for it, and generally got it.

"I'll just wait for you out here. Let me know if you absolutely need me to come up and I will," Astrid said, her face creased with worry.

"All right."

I walked into the lobby. A large man stood as I entered, and boy, did he stand. He was at least as tall as Costa, putting him several inches above six feet. Where Costa was lean, this man was wide—built like a football player who did nothing but go to the gym. He wore a suit but had the guarded look of professional muscle. He wasn't exactly my type, but

I paused to appreciate the view anyway.

He watched me as I flashed my badge at the reception-ist, and then he took a step toward me, his face strangely intense, no doubt drawn by my succubus allure. I didn't have time to deal with an admirer, so I frowned at him sternly and then broke eye contact and turned to the receptionist. The woman was shaking her head. "I'm sorry, but Ms. Leigh is otherwise occupied."

"It's important police business," I said. "She's just going to have to spare me a few minutes." Not waiting for her reply, I strode toward the elevator, shooting a quick look over my shoulder to make sure the big man wasn't following me.

I glanced at the directory. NATALIE LEIGH, WITCH was listed in suite 1400. I stepped into the elevator and hit the button for the fourteenth floor.

Astrid's partner, Claude, was a vampire, and in addition to working for the police department, he was the unofficial attaché between the local vampire leader, the Magister, and the local cops. Between Astrid's dislike for witches and Claude's vampire status—vampires and witches didn't get along well—they probably avoided Natalie like the plague. Lieutenant Vasquez probably loved them for it. Witches were tough on the department's budget.

The doors dinged open and a plush hallway revealed itself. I walked to Natalie Leigh's office door. Voices mur-mured inside, and I heard the *click* of a telephone being re-placed on its cradle as I swung the door open. The reception-ist warning the Covenant witch of my impending arrival, no doubt.

The reception area was empty, but the door to the single office in the suite was half-ajar. I walked to it and knocked lightly. The hinges creaked slightly as I pushed it open.

A dark-haired young woman—younger than I would have guessed a fully certified Covenant witch could be—stood behind the desk. She was short, probably just above five feet tall, which made her slightly taller than Astrid. She was pretty in the same way Astrid was—a cute pixie face with a short cut that only looked really good on very pretty women—but she possessed an air of sophistication that Astrid lacked. Where Astrid was down to earth, girl next door, Natalie was the understated movie star or politician's daughter. Her height made her more than half a foot shorter than me, but thanks to the man sitting across from her desk, I wasn't the giant in the room.

"Detective," Natalie said, voice smooth despite the palpable tension in the room. "I understand it was important for you to speak with me immediately, but I'm afraid I'm in the middle of something—"

"Nonsense," the thin man said. "Please see to the detective, Natalie. I can entertain myself for a few minutes."

He was a slight man, but well dressed and manicured. Over six feet tall, he was thin as a rail, something his height only accentuated. Balding, he had smoothed his dark brown hair back from his face and held it with gel. The lights glinted off his cold blue eyes.

"I'm Detective Marisol Whitman," I said, and I reached out to shake Natalie's hand.

The man's spine stiffened, making his posture almost too perfect. Great. He'd probably just picked up on the fact that I was a succubus. Men tended to have one of two reactions to my nature. They were either very interested—like the big guy in the lobby—or very irritated. Control freaks especially

didn't appreciate my innate ability to distract them. No wonder I bothered Costa.

Natalie nodded to me. "This is Councilor Koslov."

"Nice to meet you," I said smoothly. Wonderful. A Covenant Councilor. Just what I needed to complete my day. I
reached out to shake the Councilor's hand. "I'm so sorry to
interrupt your meeting."

"Nice to make your acquaintance, Detective," Koslov
said, his voice the perfect professional pitch. He took my
hand in his, shaking it, and I found myself studying him. For
such an unremarkable-looking man, he had a bit of an aura
about him. He was attractive in the way powerful men were,
and he commanded attention. To my chagrin, I realized I was
staring, and I glanced away. Damn politician. No wonder he
was on the council. He had that bit of charisma that all the
best statesmen possessed.

"We can speak in my reception area." Natalie gestured
to the room I'd walked through to get to her office. "I'll be
right back, Viktor."

The man nodded, a solemn expression on his face. I
wondered if he practiced it.

Just as Magisters oversaw their pockets of the world and
ruled the vampires, the Covenant was run by Councilors.
Unlike the Magisters who were appointed, Councilors were
elected and ruled all witches in their area of the world. Six
councils in all ruled them.

I might as well have interrupted her meeting with the
secretary of state or the vice president.

Natalie cleared her throat and I jumped. Heat flushed
my cheeks when I realized that I'd been staring at the councilman. I turned quickly and followed Natalie into her small

waiting room.

"Okay, what is this about?" Natalie asked, shutting her office door behind her.

"We have some remains," I replied. "A body was burned beyond all identification. We've determined no accelerant was used. We need to find out what else could have burned a body so badly, and whether or not you can get anything off the body to help us identify the victim."

"How badly was the body damaged? Tell me about the circumstances," Natalie said.

"Only ashes remained," I explained. "Mostly. A few more minutes and we wouldn't have been able to determine the ashes were human without a sensitive. Not even enough was left of the teeth to be certain it was a human being." I took a deep breath. "But it was enough to get the para-normal unit out there. Our sensitive verified the ashes were human remains, or an otherworlder. There is definite energy on the body that is OW in nature, but she can't say for sure if it's from the victim or the person who burned the body. And there's not enough of it left for Astrid to identify what kind of otherworlder was involved."

"Astrid Holmes?" Natalie asked, voice sharp.

"Yes," I said.

"Guess she didn't want to come with you to talk to me."

"She's working other leads in the case," I lied.

"Humph. Sure she is." Natalie pursed her lips. "Well, I probably can't tell you who the victim was, not off a little ash. You might do better with a psychometrist. But I can tell you what could have destroyed the body." She held up a finger. "A witch, for one. A not-so-strong one with an affin-ity for fire could have done it, perhaps. Especially if intense emotion was involved. A powerful one with no affinity for fire could have done it as well—although that would have required a lot of time and trouble." She held up another finger. "A salamander. But it would have to be a strong one." And another finger. "A firebird—but again, it would have to be an especially strong one. Was there damage to the surrounding area?"

"No, the damage was concentrated on the body itself."

"Probably not a firebird, then. They aren't all that accurate."

"What about a phoenix?"

Natalie waved her hand in the air. "That's just another word for firebird—they're the same species, really. They just won't admit it. I guess it could also be some sort of elemental shaman. They're similar to witches, but their magic is far more…primitive."

"Anything else?"

"Not that I can think of offhand."

"What can you tell me about salamanders?" I asked, keeping my tone light. I was only curious because of the case—not because of Costa. And if I told myself that enough times, maybe I'd believe it.

She shrugged. "Like all species of otherworlders, they vary in strength, but they are more accurate than a firebird. Most commonly they are fire resistant—maybe closer to immune. Their eyes turn black like a true salamander's when they are feeling intense emotion. Most are like a lighter, in that they can start a small flame. They can drive some energy into a fire." She shrugged. "But melting fillings…how long did this person burn?"

I frowned. "It's hard to say, but it couldn't have been

more than an hour or so. He or she was found in an alley at night, but the bar that used the Dumpsters closed at 2:00 a.m., and they took their trash out after closing. A bakery on the other side of the alley had workers in by four. They found the body at four thirty, and it was already reduced to smoldering ash."

"Sounds like you definitely have something, then." Natalie's face scrunched, a cute expression on her, and oddly it reminded me of Astrid's expression back in the alley when she had been concentrating on using her sensitive powers on the pile of ash. "If I had to hazard a guess, I would put my money on an amateur witch with very strong fire acumen."

"Why not the others?" I asked. "Seems like a Covenant witch would be just as likely."

Natalie laughed, a light musical sound. "Oh, I won't argue with you that a Covenant witch would be more likely to have that kind of juice, but our numbers are limited. Besides, Viktor has been in town all week. No way would one of ours try to pull something like that with a council member in town. That would be...suicide. Professional suicide, of course."

Professional suicide. Yeah, right. More like physical homicide when the councilman got ahold of the witch. Like the vampires, the Covenant tended to take care of their own problems.

"And," Natalie added, "a very powerful salamander could have done it."

Her points were valid, but they didn't really eliminate any of the species she'd named, just made some more likely than others. Hell, Mac had found that out only months before. Incubi, cousins to my species, were supposed to be extinct. Mac had discovered not one, but two of them on that case. One of which was a deranged killer, and the other she was currently living with. The fact that powerful ones were somewhat rare sure as heck didn't take them off the potentials list if *extinct* didn't.

My thoughts briefly flitted to Costa. He was a salamander, after all. I didn't think it likely he'd come into town early to burn some poor person behind La Maison, but I'd have Vasquez check his whereabouts to be sure.

"Can you get us any information from the ashes?" I pulled a small, white plastic container from my purse that Astrid had given me in the parking lot. It was enclosed in a Ziploc bag and sealed. It only looked like it would hold half a cup or so of the ash, but probably a big enough sample for Natalie.

Natalie sighed. "I can try. Not sure what I can get will be worth the amount of money it'll cost your department."

I grimaced but my voice was steady. "No amount of money is worth a life, Ms. Leigh. If what you find can help us, it'll be worth the whole of the department's budget."

Oh boy. Vasquez was going to love that.

My phone rang and I glanced at the unfamiliar number before touching the screen to answer it.

I turned away from Natalie. "Whitman." I knew it almost definitely wasn't Elaine, but my voice still caught with fear and hope.

"This is Costa. The security cameras are a no-go."

"What about her car? I saw it in the parking lot."

"We got it. But it doesn't look like the girls made it that far. It was locked up tight. The CSIs are going to go over it anyway, but I don't think it's likely they'll find anything."

I cursed under my breath. "This is what you called to tell me?" I winced. I was directing my worry for Elaine into anger at Costa. I knew that, but I couldn't seem to help myself. He'd been kind of a jerk earlier, though, so that soothed my guilt a bit.

He hesitated. "There's something else, but I think we're better off talking in person."

I stifled a sigh. "Fine. Where are you?"

"I'm at the Hampton, off Illinois Street."

"I know where that is." I glanced at Natalie. "Not sure how long I'll be, but I'll be there." I tossed my phone back into my bag.

"Was there anything else, Detective?" Natalie turned to head back into her office as she spoke.

"How much for a locator spell?"

The witch turned back to me and smiled, and I'd swear I saw dollar signs flash across her eyes.

Costa's hotel was on the north side of Chicago. It was probably the closest to the police department within the OWEA's budget.

A quick call with Vasquez from my car confirmed Costa's whereabouts when our alley victim was incinerated. He had an ironclad alibi—it was hard to beat the word of a dozen cops and a DA. I trudged to his room and knocked briskly on the door. It swung open and I took a quick breath. A light sheen of moisture reflected off Costa's naked chest and he rubbed his wet hair with a towel. He stepped back, and I caught the door automatically before it could close behind him.

I followed him into the room and kept my eyes firmly affixed to his muscular back. It was tempting, but not as tempting as the tight butt I could see the outline of in his jeans.

"Just a minute," he said. He reached the bed and tossed the towel onto a desk situated across from it. As he grabbed a T-shirt out of the suitcase sitting on top of the bed, I swallowed. I did my best not to reach out and run my fingers down his hard chest while he pulled the material over his head.

As he straightened his T-shirt, I licked my lips and met his intense gaze. I knew that the heat I felt was plain to see on my face, but his expression didn't harden, it smoldered. His nostrils flared, like he was an animal who'd caught my scent, and I blinked in surprise.

I took an involuntary step back and dropped my eyes. "Sorry," I mumbled. I wasn't entirely sure what I was apologizing for, but it seemed like the right thing to say. It was the only thing I could think of, anyway.

"I, um..." He cleared his throat. "Just needed to get in a quick shower. You were longer than I expected.

I took a deep breath, air through my nose, slowly out my mouth. "I tried a locator spell with Natalie. She's the Covenant witch the department uses."

"And?"

Business. Focus on business. Focus on working the case. Focus on finding Elaine. "No dice. She's either blocked by magic, out of Natalie's range, or..." The thought that Elaine might be dead stomped out the last bit of my lust. "What's this information you couldn't give me over the phone?"

Finding bravery in my resolve, I looked back to his face. His expression had hardened to its normal cold calculation. None of the fire remained, and I suddenly wondered if I'd imagined it. No. I was a lot of things, but sexually unobservant was not one of them. As a succubus I had an inhuman grip on my sexuality, and that of those around me. It was my natural gift, my natural weapon.

My natural curse.

I didn't think about it much, anymore. But standing in front of him, I wondered if my aura of sexuality affected him. Well, it almost certainly did on some level—the aura wasn't something I could turn off—but he might be able to ignore it, for the most part. After all, it didn't make me that much more noticeable than your average attractive woman, just a smidgeon more—just enough to make me a bit more distracting than most.

"I owe you an apology."

My eyes widened, and red crept up his neck.

"I made a bad assumption, about you flirting with the security man. That wasn't fair of me. I know that you have to use what you've got to get information from people in this business." He shook his head and a bit of damp hair clung to his forehead, and I made a fist to avoid reaching out to brush it away. "It makes sense, your approach. I just…reacted."

I nodded, unable to speak for a moment, and a strange feeling spread through my chest. "Do you have something against succubi, Costa? Or do you *just react* that strongly to all the people you work with?"

He flinched. "That's none of your business."

"I think it is. If we're going to work together on this, I need to know that I can trust you to have my back."

His face reddened. "You can trust me, but I'm not going to get into my fucking personal business with you."

Oh yes. Valerio Costa had some personal issues with my species and me. I frowned at him but didn't push. The likelihood of him confiding in me now was somewhere between zero and none.

"Look, I'm sorry for how I reacted earlier." He cleared his throat and gestured toward the desk. "Maybe you should sit down."

"Come on, whatever you tell me can't be any more shocking than that apology." I gave him a small smile, but he didn't return it. Instead, he ran his fingers through his hair and looked down. I shoved my chin farther up. "I'm fine. Just spit it out, please."

"It's Wendy." He reached forward and grasped my shoulder, and for a brief moment I wanted to lean into that grip, into his body. Let someone comfort me for once. But I couldn't do that. For one, he'd almost definitely push me away. For another, it was too dangerous. Comfort too easily led to other things. So I tried to focus on what he was saying, clinging to Wendy's name like a life raft.

"Wendy?"

"I'm sorry, Marisol. She's dead."

Chapter Six

"She's—" My voice caught in my throat, and I tried to swallow around the lump that had formed. A deluge of feelings crushed me, and I couldn't breathe. Wendy was dead. Gone. The brave girl who'd defied her parents and culture to attend college. The smiling friend who'd helped bring Elaine out of her shell. The understanding siren who'd helped make my sister whole.

Costa pulled me close and wrapped his arms around me in an inescapable hug. I struggled to breathe evenly. I couldn't lose it, not now.

"Elaine?" I gasped out.

"No sign of her yet. I'm sorry, but that's a good thing. Really. She's out there and we're going to find her."

I didn't move for a few moments. For those brief seconds I leaned against his hardness and took in his clean scent. I hadn't known Wendy all that well, but she had been a regular visitor to our house lately. She'd always been kind to me and as far as I could tell, to Elaine. And by helping Elaine, by becoming her friend, she helped me more than the sweet siren could have known. She alleviated the pressure of being the only one to care for Elaine, the only one who tried to bring her out of her shell. And for that, I loved her.

I pressed my hands against Costa's chest and pushed myself back. I could feel the heat of his skin beneath his shirt, and it struck me that for once, he wasn't cold. I steeled myself and met his gaze with as level a look as I could summon, ignoring the wetness I could feel on my cheeks that now marred his otherwise dry shirt.

"How do you know she's dead?" I asked.

"That's complicated."

"Complicated? You haven't told me everything," I said. It wasn't a question. "You're going to tell me what you know. Now."

"Look, there are things I can't—"

"Now, Costa!" My voice cracked and he took a step toward me. I waved him off.

He sat down heavily on the bed and rubbed his face. "Fine. Sit down," he said.

I pulled the office chair from the desk and turned it to face him. I sat, keeping my posture straight, careful not to lean toward him. I had to concentrate, keep my mind on finding Elaine.

"We've recovered one succubus out of who knows how many that he's taken."

I took a deep breath. "He?"

"Yes, she confirmed the kidnapper was a man, but she couldn't recall what he looked like. A spell, we suspect. But if he used a spell, it was clever enough that our Covenant witch couldn't undo it."

"Not surprising," I said, relieved that my voice sounded far stronger than I felt.

He blinked at me. "What do you mean?"

"Magic's a helluva lot easier to do than undo. I mean, if her memory were wiped, it would be like cleaning a car. Even though you knew the mud was there, could find it in the drain it washed down, you still couldn't paint it back onto the car and make it exactly how it was before you cleaned it."

He pressed his elbows against his knees and leaned forward. "That's what our witch told us. But it took him two hours and a fucking whiteboard to explain it."

I shrugged, uncomfortable. "I studied witchcraft, amateur stuff mostly."

"Why?"

I shook my head. "Elaine had some bad history. I just...I tried to find a way to undo it."

He gave me a quick nod. "I read the file."

My eyes were suddenly moist again, and so I examined the wall to his left.

"Anyway. The girl we rescued had been sold to a man—a human. We recovered her because his private plane was randomly searched as he was leaving the country."

I snapped my head back to him. "What? A human couldn't control a succubus—even a weak one—for long. I mean, it might take her a few times but eventually she'd drain him if he touched her. That doesn't make any sense."

He rocked back on the bed, stretched, and resumed sitting. I tried not to notice the muscles moving under his shirt. That was more difficult—now that I knew what they felt like under my hands.

"She'd been altered."

"Excuse me?"

"Magically." He took a deep breath. "Basically, someone figured out how to reverse the normal succubus process. Instead of being able to pull power into herself from the person she was sleeping with, she was able to give it. And—"

"And?" There was more? Wasn't this bad enough? I could barely get my mind around the implications.

"They removed the…baggage that usually comes along with bonding with a succubus."

"Baggage? You mean the emotional connection, the feelings." My shock twisted, and suddenly I could barely breathe, I was so angry. "They made them into fucking human batteries, that's what you're saying? Human batteries to be raped and used and sucked dry?" The sympathy that flashed in his eyes was too much. "And you knew this. You knew this and didn't tell me. What the hell, Costa?"

"I'm sorry," he murmured. "I didn't think it would help, and I didn't want to distract you from the case. We still have time to find her. We will find Elaine before they do this to her."

I opened my mouth, to yell or to cry, I wasn't sure which. But his words stopped me. "What do you mean?" My voice was thick with emotion, and I couldn't seem to get a grip on it. I had to. Had to force it down, keep focused. Had to find Elaine.

"The process—the change, it takes weeks. Weeks where the succubus can't be moved and is held in the same city she was taken from. I think she's still here, Marisol."

"You found this out from the succubus you saved?"

"Yes. She recognized the area she was held in, an old warehouse in her hometown — St. Louis. She knew she hadn't been moved because it sounded like her home, smelled like it. She grew up not far from where they held her."

"You were able to track down the warehouse?" I shifted in my seat. Yes. This was good. Evidence I could concentrate on, use it to focus.

"Yes, we found it." He frowned. "But it didn't actually lead us anywhere. The warehouse was owned by a large company and just rented out under the table for cash."

I pressed on my temples. Something wasn't right about this. Companies didn't do that, did they? "Was there anything fishy about the company?"

"Only that it was owned by your very own local Magister."

The headache just starting in my temples pulsed harder. "We should talk to someone at his company."

"I've been working on setting that up, but it's a long shot, since it was rented under the table. The Magister probably never even knew about it. But it can't hurt to try to get his records."

Great. Yet another thing he hadn't deigned to mention. And getting the Magister's business records? Fat chance. "So how was she changed? Witchcraft?"

"That's what we figure."

"To pull something like that off...I mean, that's complex magic, Costa."

He pushed up from the bed and stalked across the room to the small mini-fridge in the corner. "I know." He grabbed a paper sack from the top of the fridge and tossed the bag, revealing a small bottle of whiskey. Quirking his eyebrow, he held it up. An offer.

I shook my head and he shrugged. Grabbing a plastic hotel-provided cup, he said, "It either has to be a Covenant witch behind this, or one of the stronger underground anti-Covenant groups." He poured a couple of shots into the plastic cup, sans ice. "At this point, I'm not sure which would be worse." He downed the whiskey in one quick motion.

My stomach dropped. A witch strong enough, clever enough, to twist an otherworlder's powers. Not only strong enough, but willing to do so for money. Dangerous didn't begin to describe such a person.

"Right now, we're operating under the official assumption that this is the work of an underground group, perhaps led by an excommunicated Covenant member. It's more likely than an individual. A coven of witches with enough power to pull this off isn't a stretch."

I nodded. "And if they were led by a person with Covenant training..."

"Exactly."

"I didn't even know that they excommunicated members. I mean, I'd heard that they don't always accept every Covenant family member, but not about that."

"It's rare." He poured another double shot and grimaced. "They may not allow a Covenant family member to join for a few reasons; the most common, as you probably know, is a lack of power. They blame it on diluted bloodlines, but it happens in the pure families as well. Genetics always tosses one out there with a weak magical capacity. But excommunication is different." He tossed back the shots and let out a small cough. "They excommunicate for crimes against the Covenant, ones that aren't severe enough for execution."

I raised an eyebrow. "Such as?"

He twisted the lid back onto the whiskey bottle and set it on the fridge. "I don't know, really. I could hazard some guesses, though. Stealing, putting the Covenant in a bad public light for not following their rules. They're very twitchy about outsiders getting into their business, so I don't know for sure."

I took a deep breath and let it out slowly. "You've known this all along and you didn't share it with me. What happened to giving me all the case information, Costa?"

"I did it for your own good. You were already under enough pressure with Elaine." He glanced wistfully at the bottle on top of the fridge.

"Another fucking lie. You didn't tell me because you didn't trust me. You proved that when you accused me of going after the head of security. What the hell do you have against succubi?"

His eyes seemed darker than normal, and it was almost as if the whites of his eyes had disappeared. I tried to clear my vision. His eyes were normal again. A trick of the light? No. That was what Natalie had meant by their eyes taking the characteristics of true salamanders. I stared back, unflinching.

"It's personal." He looked at the floor, and his jaw muscle clenched. "Let's just say I don't place a lot of trust in succubi." He closed his eyes for a few seconds before turning his gaze back to me. "I won't lie to you again."

My stomach wound itself into a tight knot. He either told me the truth or he didn't. Forcing him to tell me everything he knew wasn't something I could do, and badgering him the whole night for his life story was hardly a productive way to spend my time. For whatever reason, he didn't trust succubi. I'd bet my salary that one had broken his heart way back when, and apparently the man couldn't let it go. "Is that everything you know?"

"Yes."

"You'd better not be lying to me." I got up from the chair. "You know, there is at least one very powerful Covenant member in town this week. Viktor Koslov."

"The council member?"

"Yes."

"Interesting. Something to check out, maybe—very quietly. But I don't see a council member being involved in a crime like this."

I brushed a chunk of hair from my eyes. "Why not?"

"Well, for one, they tend to be from old, very wealthy families. That would remove the money motivation, and I'm not sure why else someone would be selling succubi. Killing, sure, if they hated the species or women in general. But selling them?" He shrugged.

I frowned. "I can't really think of another motive off-hand, either, but I don't think we can write him off."

He nodded and reached into a laptop bag that was propped at the edge of the bed. "Here." He gave me a stack of folders as thick as my fist. "Copies of our full files."

I reached out and grasped the folders, but he didn't release them. I met his hard gaze and blinked.

"We will find her, Marisol."

I took a deep breath and tried to clear my thoughts. "Okay. So where is Wendy?"

"We don't know yet."

"Pardon?"

"We sent a sample of her DNA, in addition to some

personal objects, back to my partner."

My mouth dropped open. "I wasn't aware psychometrists could do that. I thought they just got images, pictures from objects. Most generally unrelated to crimes. Well, I've heard of them getting crime-related images off murder weapons and such, but not random items."

"That's true, but my partner has better luck getting useful information from objects than your average psychometrist. She saw Wendy's death from her hair sample. The other objects only gave her old memories, unrelated."

I took a step toward him. "Did she get a look at the killer?"

"Not really. She got a flash of an arm, some sort of sleeve tattoo, but she couldn't see any details. Wendy was... Well, she'd already been beaten pretty severely at the point where the vision started."

I swallowed around the lump in my throat and kept my eyes on his chest. "Tell me everything she saw."

"Beatrice could barely see through her eyes; everything was blurred. Not just the normal blurring because of the psychometry, but—"

"Yeah, I get it." Her eyes were probably swollen, maybe injured.

"There were two men in the room, Beatrice is certain of that much. One with the tattoos down his arm, and the other she never saw. But while the tattooed man held Wendy, the other man did something to her neck. It was painful, Bea said. And she thinks that's what killed her." He reached out and pushed my hair behind my shoulder. Then, letting his arm fall slowly, slid his hand from my shoulder to my elbow.

"A vampire? Could it have been a vampire at her neck?"

"She couldn't be sure. But yes, that's possible."

"We need to find Wendy's body."

The unbearable silence of the almost empty police department threatened to suffocate me, so I spread Costa's files across my desk as soon as I got there and started to go through them. I grabbed a soda from the vending machine and a candy bar and called it dinner, eating and drinking while I read the files. But the words on the pages only seemed to confirm what Costa had told me. The OWEA knew exactly jack about these kidnappings.

Oh, they'd managed to track down other possible victims—succubi from Los Angeles to New York to Denver, one in Anchorage, even—but they seemed to have almost nothing else to go on. The women disappeared from their homes, their jobs, their schools. Most were young—under thirty. That made sense. Top dollar would be paid for the young ones.

I massaged my neck and tried to think. The asshole selling the succubi was smart. He seemed to leave no trail. And he was getting braver. For the last two years he'd been taking women, but no more than one per month. The last three—including one in Anchorage, one in Phoenix, one in Chicago—had been taken within three weeks of each other. Had he streamlined his process to change them? If so, he might plan on selling Elaine and moving her out of the city faster.

I looked through the city list again, memorizing it. Memorizing the girls' names.

When I ran out of soda, I bought a ginger ale, deciding I might as well give myself a fighting chance at some sleep. A brief worry flitted into my mind while I listened to the bubbles fizz. I was a succubus, too. But no. I was too old. And I was a cop. No way would they be stupid enough to come for me. And whoever was behind this wasn't an idiot.

It almost had to be a witch. Nothing else could hope to bend powers like that. Hell, if Costa didn't have the succubus they'd rescued, I would have said it was impossible even for a witch. I tried to wrap my mind around a power twisting like that, and I wondered if they only warped the conscious part of the succubus powers, or if they warped the unconscious part, too.

I spun around slowly in my chair and tried to imagine a nonsuccubus with succubus powers, ignoring the sidelong look one of the uniforms gave me. One chuckled, and I resisted the urge to make a rude gesture toward him the next time I spun his direction.

I'd almost never tapped into my conscious powers—the ability to pull energy from others and thrall. In fact, I'd never taken power from someone before. The risk was too great, and it connected the succubus to the person she took the power from. That was risky in all but the most solid relationships. I'd played a bit with thralling when I was younger, but my attempts were meager. Succubi who didn't pull power from a mate didn't have much juice.

I stopped turning in my chair long enough to take a quick sip of ginger ale, then resumed my slow spin.

But what about my unconscious powers? Those I used on an almost daily basis—mostly to get information from suspects. But they also impacted every situation I ran across that involved other people. I couldn't be separated from the aura that differentiated me from the average sexy woman, giving me that touch of other. It was built into me, into my very DNA.

Could the witch actually be messing with that part of the succubus power as well?

I stopped spinning, an abrupt wave of nausea washing over me. Even the idea of taking the powers of another person was sickening. Might as well take their skin and wear it like some sort of creepy serial killer. Only not as obvious, and infinitely more difficult to trace.

How could such a witch be tracked down? The Covenant wouldn't give us any information about members without an ironclad warrant, and no way would a judge give us one that would encompass the entire organization's roster. Chances were the witch wasn't Covenant, anyway. They monitored their members too closely.

I swallowed the last of my ginger ale and tossed the can into the trash bin next to my desk.

A group of witches made sense. They would have more power than a single witch, and if they were led by some sort of twisted magical genius...

I frowned. Grabbing my bag, a feeling of dread and dismay overwhelmed me. Was it possible? I took out the single file remaining in my bag. Astrid's case. An otherworlder had been burned by either a witch or a salamander or a fire-bird—but most likely a group of witches. How likely was it that more than one powerful witch, or group of them, was running around Chicago?

Could the cases be connected?

Costa looked little worse for wear the next morning, and in fact, appeared annoyingly well rested. He sat across from me in the booth of my favorite breakfast place and flashed me a hesitant smile before nodding at the waitress when she asked if he wanted coffee.

"My, aren't we perky," I muttered bitterly.

That got me a real smile, which I promptly glared at.

"Not much rest, huh?"

I shrugged and he nodded. "Yeah, I wouldn't have expected you to."

The waitress delivered my hot water and an array of teas, along with Costa's coffee.

"What can I get y'all?" she asked.

"Fruit and yogurt. Oatmeal," I said.

"Give me your ham and cheese omelet." Costa gave the waitress his menu and took a sip of his coffee.

"So," I said, plopping an Earl Grey tea bag into the hot water. "I have a theory."

"Oh?" His eyebrows rose.

I pulled my tea bag in and out of the hot water. "Well, not exactly a theory; let's call it a loose idea."

He snorted. "Okay, what is it?"

"Astrid and I have a case—well, it's really her and Claude's case, but he's out of town so I've been helping her." How to explain it? The theory had sounded so reasonable to my muddled brain the night before, and it still made sense. But getting it out in a way that didn't sound nuts was difficult. "Remains have been found, but they're so badly burned they required Astrid's skill as a sensitive to even be able to identify them as otherworlder. The person who was burning them seems to have done a marvelous job. If they hadn't been interrupted, the body probably wouldn't have been identifiable as human within a few more minutes."

His grip tightened around his coffee cup ever so slightly. "Yes, I remember the case. And?"

"And after consulting a witch, we've narrowed down the species that could do that sort of thing—there aren't many."

I took a sip of my tea and watched him over the rim. He was tense, almost imperceptibly, but it was there. Were there other things he wasn't telling me? Did this fit some theory he already had, some evidence he'd already found?

"We've narrowed it down to a very powerful witch, a salamander, or a group of less-powerful witches. A firebird or shaman is also a possibility, but they're a little less likely. The scene was too neat for a firebird, and our witch source thinks that a shaman probably wouldn't be strong enough."

His jaw clenched tightly but he kept his expression only vaguely interested.

I watched him closely. "A powerful witch is unlikely, and salamanders aren't uncommon. She thinks it's likely a group of witches. Maybe the same group that's kidnapping these succubi."

A hint of amusement touched his features. "Your witch hasn't met that many shamans, apparently."

"Why do you say that?"

"I've met a few through cases I've worked on. They can be pretty damn powerful. But no Covenant witch is going to want to admit how powerful they can be. It's a matter of pride." He rubbed his face. "I'm sorry, but I don't see how the cases could be related. Just because the same group or person might—*might*—be capable of both crimes doesn't connect them. It's a huge reach."

We fell into silence for a few minutes. He ignored my glares, and I tried to think through my theory. It fit. Sure, it wasn't ironclad, but that didn't mean we shouldn't explore it. Finally, the waitress broke our standoff as she delivered his omelet and my healthier meal.

I tried to drop the subject, but it pressed against my mind, my tongue. And Costa seemed to be enjoying his omelet far too much for how angry I was. "What do you mean, that's a huge reach?" I hissed. "When the list of potential suspects is so small, and both crimes are happening in my city at the same time, that's a good reason to think they might be connected." I scooped up a bite of fruit and glared. Granted, there was only a small chance that the crimes were connected, but even a small chance was too enticing to ignore when we had so few leads. Besides, that didn't make the theory a huge reach. A stretch, sure. But he was making it sound like I was grasping at straws.

"I mean that it's a reach. Sorry, Marisol, but it is." He took a sip of his coffee and then looked down at his omelet.

I didn't reply, and instead ate my oatmeal on autopilot while trying to think. This wasn't a silly lead—and if it was a reach, it wasn't an outlandish one. Heck, we didn't have any other great leads to follow.

"You don't want to follow up on this because you really don't see a possible connection, or because it might get one of your buddies in trouble?" I asked. I knew Costa couldn't be directly involved, the dates just didn't line up. He wasn't in Chicago in time to have burned our victim in the alley.

He let out a short laugh. "Yes, because all salamanders know each other. Just like you know all the other succubi."

I waved my hand. "Point taken. Okay, if you don't think there's a connection, maybe you could still help me out."

"Do tell."

"How difficult would this be for a salamander? Burning a body—bones and teeth and all—in a couple of hours."

He leaned back in the booth and sipped his coffee. "Not easy. I'm not sure I could do it, and I'm no slouch in the fire production department," he said, voice matter of fact. No arrogance touched his tone. Interesting. "Salamanders are like most oh-dubs. They vary in power and ability. Me, for example…"

"What about you?"

"I'm pretty strong in the fire creation area—probably ninety-fifth percentile, if one measured such things. But I have very low resistance to fire."

I raised an eyebrow at that and took a sip of my tea.

"Oh, I'm not saying I'm quite as susceptible as a human, but I'm pretty weak compared to other salamanders." He leaned forward and stared at me with his dark and intense gaze. "If you light me on fire…"

My breath caught in my throat. Realizing I was leaning toward him, I grimaced and moved back. "So you burn."

"Yes, which is depressing for someone so good at making fire." Amusement traced his expression and I barely refrained from rolling my eyes at him like Elaine had done to me so much lately.

"Sorry that your pyromaniacism is so limited."

The mock sadness that touched his expression made me grin. I finished my breakfast and drank the rest of my tea.

Costa glanced at his watch. "We need to get going."

"Where to?"

"I got us an appointment," Costa said. The waitress took the bill along with Costa's credit card. I tossed some cash on the table for the tip and made a mental note to cover our next meal.

"An appointment, huh? Sounds nefarious. With whom?"

"The local head vampire. The Magister."

Chapter Seven

Costa drove his rental while I played with his radio and thermostat settings. He glanced at me a few times, and even though it was difficult to see his expression behind his sunglasses, I would have sworn there was amusement in his eyes, despite his annoyed tone when he asked exactly how old I was, and if I really thought a woman so close to thirty should play with buttons like a twelve-year-old.

By the time we reached our destination, I was playing with the buttons for the express purpose of annoying him.

"Okay, put your big girl pants on," he said as he pulled up next to a large building that was under construction. The skeleton of the building was incomplete, and men worked on the ground to put together large steel frames.

I resisted the urge to stick my tongue out at him, and grinned, instead. "Do you really think the Magister is going to know anything useful? Not like the man manages his own operations, and I'm pretty sure whoever was in charge of that St. Louis fiasco is…retired. Vampire-style." I glanced at the building material–ridden piles around us. "And why are we meeting him at a construction site?"

"It's worth a shot to see if he's rented any warehouses in Chicago." He took a deep breath and intoned, "And we're meeting him here because apparently, one meets the Magister wherever the Magister will deign to meet."

I choked down a laugh and he raised an eyebrow at me, a small grin tugging at his lips.

"Have you ever met the Magister?"

"No," I said. "But I've heard enough."

"What's the impression you get?" Costa switched the car off and turned to face me, pulling his sunglasses down.

I shrugged. "He doesn't come off as all that impressive from what I've been told. But he has to be pretty powerful to hold three states. As far as I know, vampires don't run democracies."

"True. Anything else?"

"I'm told he seems pretty levelheaded. A bit of a politician, I guess." I pulled down the sun visor and opened the mirror. Quickly, I smoothed my hair and applied a fresh coat of lipstick. I slipped my jacket off and set it carefully between our seats. Sex appeal was unlikely to influence someone as powerful as the Magister, but it was worth a shot. "Ready?" I gave Costa my charming smile.

His eyes lingered on my bright lips for a second then he frowned and put his sunglasses back on. "Let's go."

I followed Costa over to a group of men. One was pointing at blueprints while gesturing at the building. Several others were gathered around him, most in suits, one in Carhartts that were well-worn. To my surprise, the man who had been gesturing directions from the blueprints walked to meet us, after giving the large papers to one of the suits.

He nodded to Costa and then me. His eyes only passed over me for a moment, a quick flick of his gaze, but I felt suddenly like I'd been weighed, measured, and cataloged.

"I'm Luc Chevalier. Thank you for agreeing to meet here, detectives," he said, as if we'd had a choice in the matter. "How can I help the OWEA today?"

A slightly better than average-looking man, he stood around five foot nine and had wavy brown hair and brown eyes. He was attractive, but not striking and I didn't feel the aura of fear coming from him that I usually sensed from vampires. We could have been standing outside with a regular construction foreman for all I could tell.

It was unsettling.

"Thank you for meeting with us on such short notice, Magister," Costa said. "I am Agent Costa. This is Detective Whitman from the Chicago PD's paranormal unit."

"Nice to meet you both."

A strong breeze whipped my hair around my face, and a whiff of Costa's aftershave touched my nose. I fought not to step closer to him. A man should not be allowed to smell so good.

"We're here to talk to you about one of your companies." Costa flipped open a small notebook and glanced at the first page. "NMR Real Estate, to be precise."

"I am not normally involved in the day-to-day operations of my companies, you understand. I am more of a high-level manager, but I will of course help you if I can." Chevalier's French accent coated his words, making the English sound more musical.

"Do you recall an incident in St. Louis, nearly a year ago now, where a kidnapped woman was held in one of your company's warehouses?"

Luc glanced at me. "Yes, the succubus. I remember. I never spoke with the police about it. My son, Nicolas, oversees my holdings in St. Louis. He handled the situation."

I frowned. I'd never met Nicolas Chevalier but Mac said something was off about him, and that he was quick to anger.

"Is Nicolas available?" I asked. "It would be helpful to speak with him, too."

"I'm afraid not. He left last night for Europe. He won't be returning for a few weeks." Luc offered me an apologetic smile.

"It would really help us out—" I began.

"I'm sorry, but it's impossible. He's there for important business negotiations and will not return until everything is settled. You'll have to discuss this with me."

Pressure built in my chest and I wanted to shriek and rage so badly—tell him exactly how important I found his business negotiations compared to my sister's life—that I had to close my eyes for a moment to get a grip. I filled my lungs with a deep breath of air and tried to push the thoughts riding on the tip of my tongue to the back of my throat.

"Well, then you are aware that someone at your company rented out a warehouse—with no paper trail—to an individual who used the building to keep at least one woman prisoner. An individual who then tried to ship her out of the country?" Costa asked, giving me time to compose myself.

I opened my eyes to see that Luc's attention had shifted from me to Costa, and some of my embarrassment faded, lifting a small weight from my chest.

"Yes. We had a manager trying to make some money on the side. He's been eliminated—from his position—for his actions."

I opened my mouth to ask for more details, but Costa shot me a warning glance.

"We believe that something similar may be happening in Chicago as we speak," Costa said. "We can't say for sure that this person is using one of your buildings again, but it is possible, considering how much property you own through companies in the area," Costa said.

"I find that unlikely, but you can trust that I will review my records and let you know if I see any rentals that are out of the ordinary," Luc said.

"It would be better if we could go over those records ourselves." Costa smiled, and the expression was somehow predatory.

"I don't think so, Agent." Luc's smile was just as wolfish.

"What about the manager who rented the unit in St. Louis? You said he was fired, but maybe you know how to find him," Costa shot back.

"He seems to have disappeared."

Yeah, of course he had. I didn't particularly care about the Magister's staff or how he handled his business. Right now, all I cared about was finding Elaine.

"Look." I swallowed hard as both men broke eye contact to look at me. "I understand why you wouldn't want us in your records, Magister. And really, I don't see this twisted son of a bitch going through the regular channels like that anyway. What would be more helpful is a list of the properties that you show as currently vacant that meet our guidelines."

"I'm not just going to hand over—"

"This asshole has my sister, Magister." I stared down at my hands and suppressed the urge to rub my temples. I had to convince him. For Elaine. My pride didn't mean jack right now. "I know that this isn't something you'd normally allow, but I have to find her. Please. She's been through enough."

He rocked back onto his heels and crossed his arms, a thoughtful expression on his face. I met his gaze, knowing how desperate I must look, but not caring. Elaine was more important than my pride.

"Okay," he said finally. "But only the buildings that fit your criteria."

Hope filled my chest, and I opened my mouth to thank him, but the Magister held up his hand.

"Don't thank me, Detective. My people learned from the last incident. I don't think you will find her in one of my buildings." He gave me a small smile, and for a second the average man appeared almost human. "But I do hope you find your sister."

It took less than an hour for Luc Chevalier's office to send us a list of the warehouses that met our criteria. Then another half hour back at the office for Costa and me to plot the thirty locations on Google Maps. Forty-five minutes to settle on which ones fit what we were looking for the best—far enough away from populated buildings, in areas that were run-down and not highly populated. Fifteen minutes to convince Vasquez to send a set of uniforms to check out a few of the warehouses for us.

The clock on the dashboard in Costa's rental read two by the time we headed out of the office. My stomach rumbled, but I ignored the sound. We'd already wasted too much time getting on the road. Costa didn't mention lunch, either, and though annoyed, I was grateful for it.

"So we should be able to get through two or three pretty quickly," I said. "These three are all within a mile or so of each other. I hope Chevalier's man isn't late." Chevalier had promised that one of his employees would meet us at the first location, and then travel to the other two to unlock them for us as well.

Costa grunted. I hadn't expected much more of a response. We'd been through this already, at the station. For some reason, saying it aloud made me feel better, calmer. I could deal with this so long as I had a plan.

"So your sister," Costa began.

I winced. "I'm not sure this is the best time to talk about her. I need to keep my focus."

"I get that. I know she went through some stuff—you don't have to rehash that if you don't want to. It's just... Where are your parents?" He glanced at me before returning his gaze to the road.

"We don't know who our dads are."

His eyes widened.

"Yes. We have different dads." I turned my head to face my window, and watched the gray buildings slip past us. "My mom enjoyed being a succubus. She wasn't exactly the marrying kind." My voice faded at the end, and I clenched my teeth together. It shouldn't bother me. "She passed away when Elaine was still a teenager, a couple years before..." I cleared my throat and willed the image of Elaine, so broken and damaged after her attack, from my mind. "Anyway, it's just been us ever since. I mean, we have some extended family, a couple of aunts. But they don't live around here, so we don't see them that often." My voice broke, and I blinked back tears. "Elaine is all I have."

"Like I said, I read her file. You don't have to talk about it if you don't want to."

But suddenly I did want to talk about it, and the words felt as if they would burst from my chest if I didn't get them out. "She was so damaged after the attack, I wasn't sure I'd ever get her back."

"Her date tried to rape her," he said, voice low.

"Yes, and she sucked the life out of him for it." I took a ragged breath. "And he deserved it. He would have killed her."

Costa was silent for a few moments, as if considering the right thing to say. "You know that for sure?"

"Yes. The sharing that happens when a succubus drinks from her…well, normally her lover, it allows the couple to share emotions, thoughts, even memories." Costa turned and I gripped the door, though he took the turn slowly. "Later, when she was able to talk about it, she told me that she could see his plans for her body after he was done with her. Broken and ragged and dead at the bottom of a hole somewhere."

Costa was silent, and I wondered if I was only adding to his view that succubi were dangerous. "She doesn't deserve this," I whispered. "She'd only just gotten herself back."

Costa touched my shoulder, his hand cool against my suddenly too hot skin. "We're going to find her, I promise."

The first warehouse on our list looked promising. It was in an industrial area on the south side of the city, and the exterior looked terrifying enough for a person to imagine a kidnapped girl being held there. Rust stains covered the old metal siding, and the neighborhood was quiet and dirty. Potholes pitted the asphalt that surrounded the building and the road leading to it. Bits of paper and cans traced the edges of the road.

I walked around the perimeter while we waited for the man with the key, conscious of Costa following in my wake. He moved quietly, which made me all the more aware of my heels knocking against the pavement.

"I'm going to look into that connection, you know," I told him after we'd circled the building. None of the windows was low enough to peer into, and both doors had been disappointingly sturdy. "Between Astrid's murder and our kidnappings."

He was silent and still, like a snake about to strike. His dark eyes never strayed from mine.

"So if you have something you want to tell me, you should tell me now."

Chapter Eight

Darkness crept from every corner of the warehouse, and the air hung heavily, filling my throat and lungs with moldy dampness. I coughed to clear my throat and stepped into the room, clicking on my flashlight. No power ran to the structure. It wasn't necessary since, according to Luc Chevalier, the building hadn't been used in nearly five years. And the warehouse was not available for rent because it needed to be cleaned and renovated—one among many properties on their list with that issue, apparently.

Costa's flashlight beamed from behind me, and I felt him move close—too close. I almost wished that Chevalier's man had stayed with us instead of moving on to unlock the next warehouse. I took a step, then another, walking carefully to avoid the debris on the floor.

Bits and pieces of metal were interspersed on the ground in small, cobwebbed piles. They looked like brackets of some sort—probably the last thing that was produced in this building. I moved my flashlight across the ground, revealing the large room foot by foot. The concrete floor was free of any equipment, and the warehouse looked like it was simply a big room devoid of anything to really hide behind, save some empty pallets stacked one to two feet high along the edges of the room.

"I don't see any doors leading to other rooms, do you?" I whispered.

"Looks like an office in the back," he said, voice only slightly louder than mine.

I followed him to the far side of the building, and sure enough, in one corner, a door stood. The window built into the top part of the wood was so covered in dust and grime that I couldn't make out anything in the room beyond.

Costa moved from where he stood beside me to try the knob. It turned easily.

The door drifted open and Costa pulled his gun from his belt, keeping it pointed at the ground.

"Police," he called, with a voice loud enough to carry through the whole warehouse.

Movement in the corner of the room, just on the edge of my flashlight's glow, made me jump. I pulled my gun as I hastily tried to follow the shape with the light. But I halted when I caught up to it.

"Damn rat," I muttered.

We searched what seemed like every square inch of the dirty old warehouse, but there was no basement or rooms other than the office and a couple of restrooms. Every inch felt emptier than the last and there was no sign that anyone had been in the building recently.

"She's not here," I said, as Costa pointed his flashlight

across the rafters in the ceiling.

"You okay?" he asked, turning the flashlight to face the floor.

"No, I'm not okay," I muttered, and then winced, hoping my voice was too low for him to have heard.

Costa grabbed my hand and squeezed. "If it were my brother in this situation, I wouldn't be okay, either," he said softly.

"You have a brother?"

"Yes. I have a brother."

"Older or younger?" Was it possible Costa understood more than I credited him for?

"Younger," he said, voice rough. "I am very protective of him, like you are of Elaine. I can't imagine how you're feeling right now. How you're keeping it together."

I grunted. "I thought you'd decided I was a cold bitch for handling it so well."

I couldn't see his face in the dark, but his hand dropped from mine. I fought not to reach for him, reach for the small bit of comfort that touch had given me, reach for the greater comfort I knew he could give me. If he wanted to.

"Let's just go," I said finally, the darkness and silence eating at me. "I'm fine. It was a long shot that we'd find her here. Let's go to the next one." I headed for the door, leaving Costa to follow me out, and tried to shove thoughts of Elaine trapped in a similar building—filled with dirt and rats and sharp pieces of metal—from my mind.

After searching through all three warehouses we'd pegged

for the day, I had come to the conclusion that looking for a succubus in a warehouse was akin to looking for a needle in a haystack. And that Luc Chevalier was a bit of a slumlord. We'd found exactly nothing. Zip. Nada. And neither had the other team Vasquez sent to check out a couple of other warehouses across town.

My stomach rumbled as Costa pulled up to the restaurant where I'd parked my car that morning.

"You want to go in and get a bite to eat?" Costa asked.

"Sure," I said. There were worse things to look at while I ate than Valerio Costa, that was for sure.

We walked into the restaurant and waited again for a table. A host manned the station today, a skinny young guy, who looked like he needed to grow into his long arms and legs—probably a college kid. I looked at Costa and frowned as I took in his expression. Anger creased his face into a glare. A look that he directed at the host.

I glanced at the man, but he didn't seem to notice Costa's attention. His eyes were solely focused on me, and I suppressed a sigh at the blatant look of hunger. I touched Costa's shoulder and he tore his gaze from the young man and blinked at me for a couple of seconds before his expression cleared to his normal professional visage. I didn't really notice the looks men gave me anymore, not unless they were terribly dramatic in their attention. But obviously Costa wasn't entirely comfortable with the stares.

"Are you all right?" Costa asked as we sat down at a table rather than the comfy booth we'd had earlier in the day.

"I'm as fine as I'm going to be until we find Elaine. I wish you'd quit asking me that." I flipped open the menu and my eyes glazed over reading it. Everything looked good when I was hungry.

"Sorry," he muttered. "You just seem…"

I looked at him over my menu.

A hint of a smile broke out on his face. "Okay, honestly, you look good—you always do. But you also look a little tired."

Heat traveled up my neck. "Damn right, I look good." I ignored his small prod about my lack of sleep. Of course I wasn't sleeping.

The waitress, a woman in her midforties who looked like she could do her job in her sleep, stopped by the table and looked at us expectantly. "What can I getcha?"

"Coke. Cheeseburger and fries, please. No pickles. Extra mustard," Costa said.

I trailed my eyes down the menu as she waited. Finally I said, "Fish sticks. Asparagus for the side. Oh, and hot tea, please."

The waitress made a small noise at that, but took our menus and wandered off.

"Really? Fish sticks and asparagus?" he asked, examining me like he'd never seen me before.

"I'm hungry. Everything looked good."

"So you decided to order one thing from the kid's menu and one from the adult's?"

I laughed. The sound broke from my throat before I even realized what I was doing and how inappropriate it was given my current situation. I broke off abruptly, thoughts of Elaine milling around my brain.

"You can still laugh, you know," Costa said. "It's not betraying her to not be in mourning every second of every day." He leaned back in his chair and crossed his arms. "Besides, you're beautiful when you laugh." He cleared his throat. "Not that you're not always—beautiful, I mean."

"Yeah, well, that doesn't exactly separate me from the crowd, now does it?" I said, suddenly more angry than happy about his compliment.

"Excuse me?"

"I'm a succubus," I said, keeping my voice down to avoid bringing in the whole darn restaurant into our conversation. "Beauty is sort of a given. Allure, inspiring lust in the opposite sex. It all comes with the package." I took a deep breath, trying to think through how to say what I meant. "I didn't earn any of it. It's just what I am."

His cop face returned, expressionless and cold. "I suppose."

"It's just—it doesn't make me a better investigator. It doesn't help me find my sister."

He shrugged. "It helped you convince that school's security man to be more helpful back at the library."

"Yeah, a lot of good that did us." I rubbed my temples, and we fell into silence for several minutes. When things got nearly too uncomfortable for me to stand, the waitress stopped by our table with our drinks and food.

"Look," I said, after she left. "I'm sorry. I don't mean to be bitchy, and I know you were trying to be nice."

His eyes widened slightly. "Sure. Don't worry about it."

We ate in silence. I scarfed down my asparagus and fish sticks at an alarming rate, and his burger disappeared quickly as well.

I briefly contemplated trying to convince Costa to check more warehouses with me, but the darkness seeping in the windows stopped me.

Costa pushed his plate away and took a long drink. "You should go home and get some rest."

I nodded, giving him a small smile. I agreed with him, I *should* go home and get some rest. But I wasn't going to. And considering the hard time I'd been giving him lately about honesty, it was best not to lie.

The station wasn't silent or unmanned, but the paranormal division's section was as close to empty as it ever got. Two detectives sat at their desks, their frowning faces turned toward their computers. A couple of uniforms filled out reports, looking like they'd rather be anywhere else.

I wasn't any happier to be at the station at night. I should have been safely at home, sitting in front of the late-edition news while Elaine grumbled about her homework or gossiped with a new friend on the phone. But that wasn't happening, and the station offered more access to data systems than my laptop would allow from my house, so I was stuck.

I docked my laptop and waited for it to boot up, tapping my pink fingernails on the desk while it loaded. I pondered the coffee congealing in the corner coffeemaker but decided against it. Gross after-hours coffee was more likely to give me a stomachache than wake me up.

I logged into the Illinois State Police Criminal Records Database first. There were several entries for cases that involved fire, but none of the descriptions seemed to match what I was looking for. They'd involved accelerants, and none seemed to have been burned so quickly to such a degree.

The fact that Costa was a salamander threw me, but he'd told me straight out and that garnered him some trust. I didn't consider him a suspect—well, not really. Oh, his job let him travel a lot, but unless his partner and boss were in on it, he'd hardly have time to set up a succubi smuggling ring in his spare time. Plus, he was an OWEA agent. Lieutenant Vasquez took no chances after Mac's last major case. She'd thought her partner-in-crime was an OWEA agent, and while he turned out to be one, for a while there it looked like he wasn't. Besides, Vasquez had checked his alibi. And Vasquez didn't do anything halfway.

I shot a quick glance at the lieutenant's office, but it was dark. Vasquez didn't like questions like that coming up about his department, so rules had been instituted after that case. No working with other agencies without running it by him, and all personnel were checked prior to giving out any information.

Besides, salamanders were relatively common—not everywhere you looked, but I'd bet I could find a couple on the Freak Squad roster.

A uniform who looked vaguely familiar walked up to the desk. Clark, that was it. He'd asked me out once, not long after he graduated from the academy. An otherworlder, but I couldn't remember what kind.

"Hey, Marisol," he said. "Just wanted to say that I was sorry to hear about your sister."

Tears pressed against my eyelids, and I squeezed them shut, giving Clark my back. "Thanks, Clark," I said, voice rough.

"Let me know if I can help somehow." He ignored my rudeness.

"Sure, thanks."

Clark was a nice guy. Too young for me and despite his nice form, he didn't do anything for me. But reaching out to me was kind. I shifted my focus from the young officer back to what I was doing. The federal database would take longer to load. I decided to start with the system pertaining to otherworlders only first. The data set was smaller. I couldn't imagine how many hits of burned bodies I would get from the full records.

Time ticked away on the clock above the coffeemaker as I waited for the information to load. The fed's database was always so damn slow. I tried to think through the case as I sat there, but it was difficult to focus. Instead I pulled out a legal pad and started to write down what I knew in short notes. Writing things out always made it easier for me to concentrate and make connections.

During the last two years, a lot of succubi had disappeared all over the country, from Anchorage to Phoenix and now Chicago. I thought about that, and then wrote, "Kidnapper must travel regularly" next to my notes. The kidnappers were selling the succubi to the highest bidders, no doubt accumulating a lot of cash. Would they travel in style? Probably. I made a note. What else?

I tapped the pen on the counter and then wrote, "Connected to vampires?" Chances were that the local Magister, Luc Chevalier, had been telling the truth. That he had no idea who rented the space from him previously. But it was possible he'd lied.

The information screen from the database popped up on the computer. Twelve otherworlder-related listings that matched my search parameters of occurring within the last two years and no use of accelerant. Seven of the listings were victims of house fires. That didn't mean they weren't related, but it was less likely. That left me five to check. Not bad.

The primary suspect in the first case was a woman's husband. An amateur witch, he had a very high amount of power in only one element—fire. He would fit, but he was in jail, waiting to be tried for his wife's murder. The case was active, since it wouldn't be closed until the trial was officially completed.

The next four cases were unsolved; all involved the same M.O. as Astrid's. They were all either otherworlders or killed by an otherworlder—though most, like Astrid's vic, could not be identified beyond that. Only two of the victims had actually been identified. One because enough material was left for a DNA analysis. A psychometrist had identified the other.

I clicked further into the psychometrist case first. It was probably just a coincidence. I had no real reason to think that it might be Costa's partner, but I still allowed myself a deep breath when the psychometrist was identified as a man. He worked for the Phoenix Police Department.

The victim proved to be an otherworlder. She'd been killed only three months ago, and had been gone for nearly a month before her ashes turned up. The remains hadn't been found in an alley like Astrid's victim, instead they'd been discovered in a vacant lot. A vacant lot right next to a sub-urban police department not far from Phoenix. The woman was identified as Lorna Thompson, and she'd been a siren.

The other body that showed as ID'd was found in Anchorage. There had been just enough DNA left to identify her as Mary Joyce. A twenty-two-year-old siren.

I held my breath at that. Both women were sirens. Not succubi. Could there still be a connection? The cities matched. The date ranges weren't exact, but they were close.

Maybe…just, maybe.

I printed out a few summary pages of information on all five cases that weren't tied to house fires and then typed in another search, this time for missing succubi women. The ticker slowly filled and I finally broke down and poured myself a cup of the old coffee. It had cooled, so after thirty seconds in the microwave, the gloop was ready to go. The thick liquid slid down my throat, seeming to coat my flesh as it passed.

By the time I got back to my computer, I wasn't any perkier, but it felt like a rock had settled into my stomach. The search was complete, and I sat down to go through the twenty-two results.

Disheveled was a word that I never thought I'd have the opportunity to use for Valerio Costa. But disheveled was exactly how he looked when I knocked on his hotel room door at one o'clock in the morning. He hadn't shaved before he went to bed and rough darkness formed a shadow on his face. His ruffled hair stood up in odd places, and he peered at me from behind hooded eyes.

"Are you all right?" he asked as he swung the door open.

I swallowed and tried to keep my eyes on his face. But I failed, and my gaze slid down his bare chest and boxer briefs to the long legs below, and then back up. I licked my lips. Why had I come here again?

"I think that I've found something," I said, not bothering to hide my interest in his physique. The man had a nice body under his clothes.

Costa raised an eyebrow at my frank look but didn't comment. Instead, he dressed in a T-shirt and a pair of basketball shorts. "Okay, what is it?"

"So the succubi have been kidnapped and changed. Have you given any thought to how long he had to...experiment to get that change right? What did he do with the ones he wasn't able to successfully change?"

Costa shrugged. "I don't know. I always assumed that he held whoever the first one was long enough to get it right. Poor girl, whoever she was."

"Could be," I said. "But maybe not." I waved the file folders I'd filled with my copies of the burn victims and missing succubi case summaries at him. "Maybe, like with any type of experiment—scientific or magical—they had several trial and errors first."

"Maybe. But we didn't find any bodies."

"Exactly." I strode past him into the room and tossed my purse and folder onto his bed, and then opened the folder, handing him pages as I spoke. "Three years ago, a twenty-one-year-old succubus disappears in Seattle. She's never found. But two months after her disappearance a pile of ash is discovered near a Dumpster where homeless people like to hang out. No one would have suspected anything about it, but the ash wasn't burned well enough and some bones remained."

His brow furrowed and he scanned the pages as I handed them off. "I didn't find anything about this in my research."

"That's because the ashes weren't identified as a succubus.

They were too far gone for DNA, and the sensitive they had examine them could only tell that they were otherworlder."

"That doesn't prove anything—"

I gave him the next sheet of paper. "Two and a half years ago, New York City. A succubus disappears, headed to a casting call that a friend told her about. She was nineteen years old. Three months later, ashes were found—these placed ridiculously close to a police station. Again, the ashes were too far gone to be identified as the succubus, but otherworlder energies were found on the body." I shook my head. "It's the placement of this one and several of the others that bothers me. They were all placed in spots where the person or people burning them were likely to get caught, or where the ashes were likely to be noticed as odd. Even the one here in Chicago was behind one of the nicest hotels in the city, situated by a bakery and a club so almost all hours of the day it was likely to be noticed. It's like the guy wanted to be caught."

Costa snorted. "More likely he's just trying to show how damned smart he is by taunting the police and committing the crimes under their noses."

My eyes widened. "So you think the idea has merit?"

He grinned at me. "I think this is some of the finest damned police work I've ever seen."

I shouldn't have glowed at his compliment, but I couldn't help the heat that flushed my face, or the rush of pride that filled me. I knew I was a good cop, but it felt pretty darn nice to hear someone else say it for a change. "Thanks," I said, flashing him a real smile.

He reached out and took my hand, and electricity jumped from him to me. Suddenly the room was too hot, and I took an involuntary step toward him.

His dark eyes met mine. Heat and desire rolled there, so intense that my breath quickened.

My smile faltered and he closed the gap between us. His scent washed over me—soap and toothpaste, and an underlying smell of him—and he lowered his face to mine.

He took my mouth softly, his lips cool against my hot skin. Desire rushed through me and I couldn't hear anything, couldn't see anything, couldn't sense anything but him. I wrapped my arms around his neck, pulling him closer. He slid his tongue between my lips, and I moaned.

Ringing brought me back to myself. Ringing and Costa, stepping back, pulling my arms from around his neck. Ringing, and the flash of thoughts of Elaine.

Blood rushed to my ears. I'd come here to show him what a good cop I was. To prove, for once, that I was more than sex in heels. That I was more than my succubus heritage.

And I'd ruined it.

I grabbed my jacket and purse off his bed and glanced at the files. No, I didn't need them. I had copies in my car.

"Wait a sec—" Costa said to me, phone firmly attached to his ear.

"Sorry, it's late. I have to go," I said without looking at him. Then I turned and took my sorry ass home.

Chapter Nine

My embarrassment the next day was only made worse by the fact that Costa didn't call and try to talk to me. Not surprising, really, since I'd stormed out like a shamed teenager who'd never kissed a boy before. That he didn't call me in the morning either didn't help. I knew that I should act like an adult and call him, but I couldn't. So I steeled myself and went in to the station without him. I was fully intent on ignoring what had happened between us and focusing on finding Elaine.

Then I saw him.

Costa stood next to the coffee pot with Lieutenant Vasquez, and they spoke in low tones. With his normal serious expression plastered on his face, Costa didn't look concerned at all. He appeared well rested and confident. Handsome and cool. Not at all ruffled by our kiss.

Fine. Two could play at that game.

I gave Costa a cool nod, and then headed to Astrid's

desk.

Astrid looked up at my approach and smiled at me. "Hi, Marisol. How goes it?"

I filled her in on my theory, in low tones not so hushed as to draw attention, and her brows drew together when I finished.

"That all tracks. In fact—" She opened a file drawer and grabbed a folder out of it, then flipped it open. "We just got a report in from Denver about burned remains found there. I doubt it would have been in the database yet. It's not new, but they just figured out the oh-dub connection." I shook my head and she nodded. "This one is also likely an other-worlder, found in an odd spot, right outside of the doors of a twenty-four-hour Target."

"Security cameras?" I asked.

She shook her head. "Missing footage. Quite mysteri-ously, of course."

I stilled, mind going into overdrive. Camera footage go-ing missing. That sounded too familiar to be a coincidence. No way were these people just sneaking in to steal the cam-era footage from all these places—someone would have seen something. They could only get lucky so many times. Were they buying the footage? Paying off people on the inside?

"But we did luck out," Astrid continued. She shut the file folder and met my gaze. "The killer—or killers—screwed up."

I sat down across from her and leaned toward her, reaching for the file folder. "What did we get?"

"A couple of spots of blood were found only a few feet away from the ashes, and they were untouched by the fire. We think it's our vic, and it sounds like it matches the M.O.

you're looking for. But we're waiting on lab results."

I scanned the file as she spoke. "And?"

When Astrid didn't continue I looked up from the folder, but her attention was focused above my shoulder. Great. I looked behind me and up into Costa's grim expression.

"Keep going, Astrid," I said, and turned my attention back to the folder.

"The woman disappeared around three weeks before the ashes were found. She was young—twenty-one. And she was a siren." Astrid's expression went blank and her eyes unfocused, staring at the wall behind me.

"Astrid?" The young woman didn't move at the sound of my voice. "Are you all right?" I waved my hand across the space her gaze was locked on, and she took in a deep breath.

"Sorry," she whispered, then shooting a quick glance at Costa, she said to me, "I'm headed to the lab, if you want to come."

Should I go to the lab? The large presence at my back reminded me of the benefits of accompanying her. I could avoid Costa for a while. Give myself a chance to overcome my embarrassment.

No, you put on your big girl pants today, remember? No hiding out. You're an adult.

"That's okay, but thanks. I have some other stuff I want to follow up on. But let me know what you find out, okay? I'll do the same."

"Sure," she said, but the tension in her shoulders didn't dissipate.

"Give us a second, Costa," I said, keeping my eyes on Astrid.

I could feel him walk away, though he made no noise.

I shot a glance over my shoulder. He was back across the room, standing safely next to the coffee pot. "What's wrong?" I asked her.

She stood and walked around the desk, then leaned in so her mouth was only inches from my ear, and whispered, "He feels like fire. Salamander?"

I grinned at her. "Apparently quite the wannabe pyro."

"Where are we going, exactly?" Costa asked as he shut the passenger door of my car.

I turned the key and my little Honda purred to life. "We're going to talk to Natalie, our local contact with the Covenant witches."

"You and Astrid spoke with her earlier this week, didn't you?"

"Yes, but she wasn't terribly helpful." I hit the gas and brought us into traffic. Natalie's wasn't far from the station.

"What makes you think she'll be more helpful now?" He braced himself against the doorframe as I made a quick turn.

"We're going to be more persuasive. Besides, we have more info to go on. Maybe."

Natalie Leigh waited for us in her office—alone this time. Her professional demeanor was in full force—polite smile, accommodating attitude. Until I told her why we were there.

"I'm afraid I can't give you access to our records, Detective Whitman. Even only the ones for witches who travel a lot and…" She glanced down at the note she'd jotted when

I'd started explaining what we were looking for. "…who would have the ability to burn a body to a crisp."

"Okay, then," I said. "Give me some of your expertise."

Natalie leaned back in her chair and gestured for me to continue.

"You told me that the only creatures that could burn a body without accelerant and within such a short timeframe to the degree we're seeing are salamanders, a powerful witch—or a group of witches—a firebird, or a shaman."

"Yes, to my knowledge."

"And what type of creature could twist a succubus's power to make it work in reverse?" I asked. Costa stiffened beside me. I probably wasn't supposed to hand out that case information willy-nilly, but Natalie was a good person, and she worked on plenty of secretive police cases. If I could get her to take me seriously, she might help us.

Natalie's mouth dropped open. "That's not—I mean, such a thing isn't possible."

"It's been done. To at least one succubus, and we suspect to several others." I swallowed hard. "And we think that it's being done to my sister right now. In this very city somewhere."

She glanced at Costa, who nodded.

I leaned toward her. "We need your help."

Natalie took a deep breath and then nodded. "Doing such a thing is an abomination. It's a perversion." She paused, looking lost in thought. "And such a thing could only be accomplished by a powerful witch. Knowledgeable, too. A Covenant witch."

"We think it might be an excommunicated witch," Costa said.

Relief flooded her face. "Of course. Such a thing is possible."

"Will you help us get the information we need?" I asked.

"I'll do what I can," she said, then quickly added, "but you have to keep this between us. I could lose my position for helping you without being authorized first."

I frowned. "How long would authorization take?"

She laughed, a light musical sound. "Somewhere between forever and never. There's no way the Covenant will authorize me to share this kind of information with the police. There's always the small chance that it'll be a Covenant member and they'd never willingly let anything like that come out publicly."

She was taking a big risk for us, but I couldn't for the life of me ask her not to. This was too important. Elaine's life was on the line. "How big of a list do you think it would be?"

Her forehead scrunched up as she thought about my question. "Excommunicated members? There are very few—even fewer who could pull something like this off. I'd guess less than five. Maybe only one or two that I can think of off the top of my head. I'll have to do some research." She took a deep breath and let it out in a rush. "Now current Covenant members...probably a dozen or two on the continent."

"Could a group of witches pull this off?" I didn't want to expand our potentials list, but I had to make sure we didn't miss the real perp just because we concentrated on the easy-to-track suspects.

"Maybe. But you'd still need to have a strong witch leading them. And he or she would need to have a lot of Covenant knowledge." She chewed on the inside of her lip. "No.

I think we should start with the potentials we already discussed. This kind of scheme, it doesn't seem like something a group of mediocre witches—even with a well-educated one in the group—could pull off. The burnings, yes, without a doubt. But the power-twisting…no. I just don't see it."

I hated to ask it—the man was ridiculously powerful—but I had to. "Councilor Koslov. When did he get into town?"

She considered it for a moment. "Yes, I'll admit the timing fits, but the talent doesn't."

"What do you mean?" I sat down in one of the chairs across from Natalie, conscious of Costa at my back.

"I mean Viktor could probably do it, given enough time and a good stash of ingredients, but it's unlikely. Most witches, Covenant especially, have a strength in one or two elements. They tend to nurture those powers, sometimes completely ignoring the rest. Viktor isn't a true slouch in any element—he couldn't be, as a council member. But his strength is in water. He couldn't pull off that sort of burning easily even if he wanted to." She tapped her index finger against her lips.

"How much time would he need?"

She frowned and dropped her hand to her lap. "Days, probably."

"When do you think you'll have a list for us?" Costa asked, and my chair back flexed under his grip, his long fingers only inches from my back.

Natalie grimaced. "A day or two. I'll have to reach out to some sources—discreetly. This isn't the kind of information we keep in a database somewhere."

My heart dropped, but I nodded and pushed up from my chair. I held out my hand and Natalie shook it. Costa walked to the office door and held it open for me.

"Thank you so much for your help. Finding my sister before her power is—" My voice cracked and Natalie nodded.

"I understand. I'll be in touch."

"I think we should go talk to the head of campus security again," I said when we reached my car, which was parked a good distance from Natalie's building. My refusal to pay for more than street parking had lost me many a calorie. Besides, it didn't seem fair to ask her to validate a parking ticket on top of risking her career to help us.

I half expected Costa to argue, or to ask if I had other reasons for wanting to talk to the man again, but he didn't. Instead he nodded and said, "Good idea. Something about him was off."

"Exactly. He was sweating in a cold room. And these guys, whoever they are, have a history of paying people off to get what they want. The warehouse in St. Louis where the succubus was held that you rescued? They paid a low-level vamp to rent that under the table. And the video footage that disappeared from the Target store where some of the burned remains were found, that was likely a payoff, too." I turned the car on and pulled into traffic.

"True. It would be a helluva lot easier to pay someone off to delete the footage and destroy any backups than to do some magical mumbo jumbo to get rid of it." As I made a turn, Costa's hand flew up to grip the ceiling and I grinned.

"Is it just my driving that bothers you, or other drivers in general?"

He glanced at me before his eyes moved back to the road.

I snickered and made another turn. "So, if someone is paying to have things made easier, and to make things disappear, it only stands to reason that they paid to have the video footage disappear from the library, too."

"But they could have paid off someone in security," Costa pointed out.

"True. But the security guy seemed nervous."

He nodded and we rode in silence for the next few minutes.

"About last night—"

"We don't need to talk about last night," I snapped, and then made a right turn, harder than I strictly needed to.

"I just don't want you to think that's something I do normally." He glanced at me, and something in my expression made him frown. "And I don't think it's something you do, either."

"I'm a succubus, remember? I thought you'd already decided I feed my tastes wherever and whenever I please," I said bitterly.

"I made some assumptions about you—hell, Marisol, I'm sorry for that. But I have my reasons. I already apologized. Are you going to punish me for it for the rest of the damned case?"

I chewed on the inside of my lip, searching for the right response. There didn't seem to be one. "I'm not punishing you. I just think that we both know that kissing was a bad idea. Let's just drop it, okay?" I made a hard left, but Costa's tight grip on the dash had lost its humor for me.

"Whatever you say." He turned to look out his window.

We drove in silence the last few minutes to the school. When I parked, I could almost see the tension melt from Costa's body, and I frowned.

I was a perfectly good driver.

We walked to the security office, and I glanced at the clock above the front desk. It read two. I grimaced. No lunch. Again. As if signaled, my stomach twisted in annoyance.

We walked down the hall, and I found myself moving lightly, with Costa far more reserved at my back. The idea of nailing the security guy to the wall—for helping someone kidnap my sister, no less—filled me with delight.

I rapped on the glazed glass on the head of security's door, and then opened it without waiting for a response. The man sat behind his big desk, an angry scowl on his face for our rude entrance. He looked up and met my smile, and his expression lightened. Then he saw Costa behind me, and something like fear danced across his face before the scowl returned.

"I'm sorry but I can't help you people right now. I have shift schedules for the next month that I have to finish. You'll need to schedule an appointment and come back."

Costa shut the door behind us, and the door clanked loudly as it hit. Donovan started at the noise.

The squirrely man's face suddenly enraged me, and the bit of excitement I'd felt at having a lead in Elaine's disappearance was swept away. "Where is my sister, you son of a bitch?"

His mouth dropped open. I strode around the desk, grabbed the front of his shirt, and shook him. "Where is she?" What right did he have to walk free while she was being held somewhere, scared and maybe hurt? My blood boiled, and I yelled questions at him faster than he could answer.

Hard hands gripped my shoulders and yanked me off the weasel. I fought them, until Costa turned me around to face him. "You wait over there," he said quietly, and nodded to the door.

Numbness replaced the anger, and I pulled free of Costa's grip and walked around the desk, back stiff. My professional facade had failed me. Tears burned my eyes and throat.

"We're here to talk about the money, Donovan." Costa's voice was hard.

I kept my face as emotionless as I could. We didn't have a money trail on Donovan, but he didn't know that.

Donovan shifted in his seat. "I don't know what you're talking about, but you're going to have to—"

"The money they paid you to get rid of the security footage. The money they paid you to lie to us. The money they paid you to help them kidnap a young woman," Costa said, ignoring Donovan's splutters. "You are going to tell us everything you know right now. Or you and I are going to go somewhere more private to talk." Costa leaned over the man.

Donovan cringed as his gaze met Costa's. And suddenly he pushed back, trying to scoot his chair away while never taking his eyes off the OWEA agent. "No—you can't—"

Costa slapped his palm onto Donovan's desk. "Tell us about the money!"

"Fine!" Donovan screeched. "Fine, I'll tell you!"

Costa stood straight and crossed his arms.

"A big guy came in and threatened me if I didn't help

him. And…"

"Yes?" Costa said.

"He offered me the money, too. But that's not why I did it. He was a scary guy." His eyes darted to me, but he didn't change his story. Apparently impressing me was slightly less important than not pissing off Costa. "I was worried for my life; you have to believe me!"

Costa grabbed him by the front of his shirt and yanked him up from the chair. Donovan cringed, all the wrinkles of his face suddenly visible and deeply etched, and sweat trailed down his neck to pool at Costa's hand. Costa's grip held firm, and what Donovan saw in Costa's eyes made him shake.

"Stop your sniveling." He tossed the man back down onto the chair.

"What did this man look like?" I asked.

Donovan shrugged. "Big guy. He wore sunglasses and a hat so I didn't get that good of a look. He had tattoos on his arms—they were covered with them."

I crossed my arms and gripped my elbows, trying to focus on the conversation. A sleeve of tattoos. Just like the psychometrist had seen in her vision of Wendy's death. There were so many questions I wanted to ask, but I couldn't move, couldn't speak. I shook with the force of my feelings. I knew that all it would take was one slip, and I'd be across that table, trying to strangle the evil little man. I tried to breathe, closing my eyes against the feeling.

When I opened them, Costa stood in front of me, sunglasses back on. He was shoving his cell phone into his jacket pocket. But for the life of me I couldn't remember him making a call, let alone what he'd said.

"Come on. I've got a couple of uniforms coming to take him in. We'll get an artist on the drawing tonight. By tomorrow, we should have a good idea of what this guy looks like." He lowered his voice and touched my upper arm. "Between that and the list from Natalie, we'll find this guy. I promise."

I nodded woodenly, wishing I could be so certain.

Chapter Ten

Costa took over the driving after the officers arrived to take Donovan to the station. He turned the radio on and we listened to golden oldies and hit the McDonald's drive-thru. When asked, I told him I wanted chicken nuggets and iced tea.

I blinked dumbly for a few seconds when I looked up to see us parked in front of his hotel.

"I thought we were going back to the station."

"I figured you could use a drink. It's only six o'clock. Some food and a few drinks and we can talk about the case."

He was right. And what would I do at home anyway? Sit there and feel sorry for myself, that's what. Sleep didn't seem to be a valid option for me anymore, and I would think better with someone to bounce ideas off of. "I don't really drink."

"Well, you can watch me, then."

I followed Costa to his room, carrying the drinks while

he carried the food. His room didn't have a table, but it had a small desk. I sat there and ate my nuggets, while Costa ate his hamburger on the edge of the bed. True to his word, Costa had beer and some of the whiskey I'd seen him drink before. I hated whiskey and liked beer even less, but to each their own. I'd seen cops turn to much worse things than the occasional drink—couldn't blame them with the things we saw on the job.

We ate mostly in silence, commenting occasionally about the news program on television. "So why do you think he's doing this?" I asked Costa after we'd finished eating.

Costa didn't ask who I meant. Instead he clicked off the television and faced me. "Greed, I guess. You've been a cop for a while. You know what people will do for money."

I frowned. "I get that. I mean, as much as I can. But if it was only about the money, then why move on to different otherworlders—nonsuccubi?" If my theory actually held water, that was.

"Expanding his product line." Costa sipped his beer and ignored the dirty look I shot him.

"People aren't products," I said, finally.

He rubbed his face with his free hand. "I'm not saying they are. But to some people they might as well be."

"I just—" I took a haggard breath and let it out slowly. "I'm sorry. I don't know why I'm getting emotional today. I feel like I'm going to blow up."

"Have a beer." He tossed me one and I groaned.

"Seriously? Beer is nasty." I looked at the label and grimaced.

"That's good beer. I won't have you insulting it in my house." He grinned at me and I chuckled at his stupid joke, some of the tension finally seeping out of my shoulders.

I took a sip and made a face at him. He smiled at me and my heart jumped. The man was a hottie—there was no way around it.

As if sensing my thoughts, Costa held my eyes with his own, humor suddenly gone from his expression. "My brother," he said, voice rough.

"Pardon?"

"My brother was married to a succubus. She…" He took a quick drink of the whiskey and swallowed hard. "Well, she fit the stereotype."

"That's why you were so suspicious of me? So weird about how I was acting? Just because you knew one slutty succubus?" I glared at him. "Give me a break."

Costa shook his head. "I'm sorry, but she really did a number on him. Fed from him, thralled and messed around with his friends. She even—" He stopped, took a drink from his beer. "It doesn't matter now. I shouldn't have assumed that all succubi were like her."

"She tried to seduce you, didn't she?"

He stared at his beer and his face reddened as I watched. "She got fucking close to succeeding, too." He looked up and his eyes met mine. They'd darkened to salamander black, and it was as if I could feel heat radiating from him. "My brother walked in with her wrapped around me half-naked. We haven't spoken since."

My chest constricted, and for a few agonizing moments I couldn't speak. I took in his bleak expression as he turned his attention back to his whiskey, and I finally found my voice. "It wasn't your fault. He shouldn't blame you."

"I almost fucked his wife; of course he should blame

me!" The beer bottle cracked in his grip, and he tossed it into the small trashcan by his feet.

"When succubi have fed on someone, they get power. She used her powers on you, and they would have been impossible for you to resist while you were in her presence." I kept my tone calm, but inside, my mind reeled at the idea. I'd known of succubi who would drink the essence of their partners for power and not stay with them. It was a risky practice that could lead to mental instability in the succubus. But for one to drink for a long period of time from one man and then still be willing and able to seduce and take from others?

The woman had to be a sociopath.

"You don't know that for sure." His voice cracked, as if he doubted the truth of my words himself.

"I do know. You're a lot of things, Costa, but you're not the type to seduce his brother's wife." I forced a small smile. "A bit of a wimp when it comes to being a passenger in a car driven by a perfectly good driver, but you're a good man."

Something like hope lit up his face, and his gaze turned from bleak to hungry. I slid my gaze down his strong arms, his muscled chest, and then back to his eyes. He blinked and his eyes changed again, but before I could take them in, he was pulling me to my feet and into his arms.

His lips touched mine as I wrapped my arms around his neck. Softly, his hands stroked my back, one settling on my lower back and the other moved down to graze my ass. As he tugged me closer to him I gasped against his lips. He pulled back from my mouth and held me against him. His body was so hard, and I could feel how much he wanted me as he pressed against my stomach.

He stepped back and looked at me, anything but expressionless. Tense, his face was raw with desire. I knew I looked the same to him, and I didn't care.

"I don't want to take advantage," he said slowly, as if choosing his words carefully. "This is an emotional time for you..."

"You're not taking advantage." I trailed my fingers down his chest, just grazing his shirt. "I am a succubus—"

"I know that doesn't mean—"

"Hush," I whispered. "Let me finish. The fact that you confided in me and trusted me enough to tell me what happened to you..." His expression darkened, so I pushed past the personal. "And that you followed my lead on the investigation, listened to my idea—it means a lot. Not everyone takes me seriously. Not beyond my ability to get confessions from testosterone-driven young men, anyway."

He frowned. "You're a first-class investigator, Mari."

He couldn't have said anything sexier.

I tugged on his shirt and he lowered his face for another kiss. His lips were hot on mine as he pulled me against him, but his skin was slightly cool to the touch. It seemed to grow warmer with each passing moment.

I wondered for a brief moment if this was a stupid idea, but then dismissed the worry. Whatever else he might be, Valerio Costa was a good man, and a good cop. I was a succubus, and nothing would clear my mind and make me feel better than a good roll in the hay. I wouldn't feed from him. Taking energy from another person bound them to the succubus and vice versa. It was a sharing process that connected the woman and her lover through emotion and even memory. This would be something far more fleeting—a rush to get through the sorrow.

I tugged at Costa's shirt, barely reaching the last two buttons before he yanked it off his shoulders. The white T-shirt he wore underneath soon followed, and I stopped for a moment to appreciate the view. The man was built. His height—he had to be at least six foot three inches—hid the amount of muscle he carried, making him appear lean. But he wasn't thin—far from it. I felt small standing next to him, no easy feat for a woman nearly six feet tall in her work-height heels.

Costa kissed me again before his mouth slid down my neck to kiss my collarbone and shoulder. His hands ran down my sides and back up, almost tickling in their softness. He pulled my blouse over my head, and then ever so slowly, grazed my bra-covered breast with the back of his fingers.

My face heated as he took in my sexy bra. The panties matched, and the set was like all of my underthings—pretty, overpriced, and made of very little fabric. I didn't like to flaunt my succubus nature in the open—aside from when it helped me solve cases—but I did allow myself a bit of hidden allure.

"You're so beautiful, my *bella*," he whispered, and my heart dropped.

You're more than beautiful to him, remember? And somehow, armed with that knowledge, the compliment seemed more real. Like something I'd actually earned. Like something worth mentioning.

I melted into his arms and he pulled me closer, groaning into my mouth. He made quick work of my bra and the rest of my clothes while I took off his. I wanted—needed to feel him against me, inside me.

Suddenly, we were on the bed. He was on top of me and he trailed kisses down my neck and to my chest. He took my nipple into his mouth and sucked while he massaged my other breast with his hand. Then he traced my skin as he moved his hand down, trailing heat as he slid it down my stomach. Ever so softly, he moved his hand between my legs.

When he touched me, I jumped.

"Easy," he whispered.

I could only moan in response as he palmed me, and then slid a finger into my heat. I gasped as he rubbed my most sensitive spot in a way that almost pushed me over the edge. Desperation touched me, and I suddenly needed him so badly I ached.

Could it really feel this good? The man was obviously an expert, but still. I'd never been shy about my succubus nature. I'd slept with men before—more than my fair share, probably. But with him...it was different. I could feel him, feel his energy—so close I just had to reach out to touch it, to taste him. So tempting...

The thought stilled me, and my mind whirled. I was not tempted to touch him with my succubus powers. No, I'd never been tempted, not really. Did I already care about him that much?

My racing thoughts must have shown on my face, because he touched my chin lightly and stared into my eyes. "No thinking. Just feel." He rubbed his body against mine, and I could feel his cock between my legs, brushing against my wetness. I gasped and he smiled. "Yeah, *bella*. Just like that."

He moved his mouth to my nipples, and he sucked and nibbled them until I moaned. Pulling back, he watched me as he blew on one, making me shiver, and then he took it into his mouth again. Almost rough, he plucked and rolled and sucked until I couldn't think of anything but him. Then he slid down my front, kissing and licking his way until I could feel his breath against my inner thighs. I tensed in anticipation, and he nipped at my sensitive flesh. Finally, he kissed me *there*. I gasped as his tongue touched me, caressed me, pushed me to the brink. And then lights flashed, my body tensed, and I fell over the edge, crying his name.

His chest brushed against my already sensitive breasts as he moved over me. His eyes met mine. Black, they were devoid of white cornea or pupil or iris. The mark of a salamander—the eyes that were so similar to their inhuman cousins. As he slid into me, I moaned and closed my eyes, forgetting the strangeness of his.

He moved within me, thrusting hard, in delicious rhythm that had me gasping for air and clinging to him. He reached between us and touched me, rubbing softly in rhythm with his thrusts. Stars clouded my vision and I whispered his name. He grunted and pushed into me hard, before spasming against me. I gripped the sheets and he threw back his head, calling my name.

Chapter Eleven

Costa's arms were wrapped around me when I woke the next morning. My first instinct was to burrow deeper into the covers and my second was to flee. I'm generally the sort of girl who follows her first instinct, so I snuggled a little closer. Costa murmured in his sleep and his embrace tightened around me.

The night had been magnificent and, despite the passion, I'd gotten more rest in his bed than I had on my own all week. I grinned to myself. Exercise was good for sleep.

I traced his smooth skin with my fingertips, and he wrapped his arms around me more tightly. God it felt good to be held. So good. Too good.

I blinked at the clock on the nightstand. Only seven. We needed to get a move on, but at least we hadn't really overslept. He mumbled something and took a deep breath against my hair. I smiled. No reason we had to go right now. An extra half an hour certainly couldn't hurt.

A moment passed before I processed the click of the lock giving way. By then, the door was opening. I sat up, holding the sheet against my chest, and reached over to the nightstand. I tugged my gun from its holster and pointed it at the doorway.

Or to be more accurate, I pointed my gun at the gorgeous redhead who strolled into the room, carefully balancing donuts and coffee in her hands.

We stared at each other for a moment. Her green eyes narrowed, and then she raised an eyebrow at the man next to me. Costa pushed himself up on his elbows, and he frowned at our uninvited guest.

"What are you doing here, Beatrice?"

I glanced at him. Was she uninvited after all?

"Maybe you should get your little girlfriend to drop the gun before you start asking me stupid questions, Val." Her voice was rich and smooth, and lower-pitched than I would have guessed. Sultry, that was the word.

"Put down the gun, Mari. This is my partner, Beatrice Davis," he mumbled. Costa sat up on the edge of the bed and rubbed the sleep out of his eyes.

I frowned at him but lowered the gun.

"Jesus, Val. I knew you were hoping to use the succubus to lure out the perp, but I didn't know you were going to have to fuck her to do it." The redhead grimaced and set the coffee and donuts on the desk.

My hand flew to my mouth, and self-loathing coursed through me like a vile drug sent directly to my veins. A weight settled in on my chest, and I went very still. Use the succubus? Lure out the perp? Didn't know he'd have to fuck her to do it?

"Get the fuck out of here, Beatrice," Costa said, voice low and hard. Dangerous.

Beatrice shrugged and tossed her hair over her shoulder. "Whatever, I'll be in the lobby while you two...finish up in here."

The door slammed behind her, and I flinched.

"Don't let her get to you," Costa said, voice tight. But anger didn't cover his face, guilt did. He wouldn't meet my eyes; instead he looked down. "Last time I leave a key for her. She can wait for me if she needs files from now on."

His expression carried all the confirmation I needed.

I couldn't breathe, couldn't think. I had to get out. I grabbed my clothes and yanked them on. Costa was talking to me, but I couldn't hear him. I couldn't pause to listen to his bullshit. I had to go.

He grabbed me by my shoulders. "Listen to me, *bella*."

I stepped back, staring at the floor, and he released me. I couldn't look at him. If I looked at him I would cry. And there was only so much humiliation I could take in one morning.

"Don't touch me," I finally rasped out. "You will never fucking touch me again." I shoved past Costa and ran for the door. He didn't stop me.

To my utter horror, tears started to leak down my face as soon as I reached the lobby. I moved outside quickly, keeping my head down, and silently praying that Costa's partner wouldn't see me as I shuffled through the doors. Once I hit the sidewalk, I strode to my car. Costa could find his own ride back to the station.

I hadn't cried when Elaine was taken—not really. I hadn't cried when I'd learned what they were going to do to her if I didn't find her in time and stop them. But this—crying over a man? What the hell was wrong with me? Oh sure, it didn't help that this hit on top of everything else. And the piece of my mind that remained rational realized that given all the stressors in my life—not to mention the lack of sleep—this wasn't exactly a crazy response. That it was probably a delayed reaction, having more to do with Elaine than Costa and his rude partner. But the rest of my mind thought I was shallow. And so I cried harder.

I wallowed in my misery as I drove to my house. I couldn't do anything for Elaine until I got home and calmed down, so I parked on the side of the road for a few minutes, quit fighting the tears, and let them fall.

Once I'd gotten myself somewhat together and parked in front of my townhouse, I trudged up to my front door, not even bothering to pretend I walked with any sort of dignity.

Flipping Costa.

I took a quick shower, finally letting loose the last of my tears under the hot stream of water. I let the heat wipe away the pain and anger and humiliation. I let it comfort me.

Numb, I got dressed and then made myself a cup of tea. I sat down at my dining room table. I had to focus on finding Elaine, on figuring this out. Whatever Costa had intended anyway—using me as bait aside—didn't seem to be working. The perp was either too smart to try to kidnap a cop, especially a cop working his case, or I didn't fit the bill in some other way. I wasn't exactly in the age range of the average victim—just a touch too old.

I pulled out the case files and started scanning them

again, one by one. I made a list of the cities we knew about, and approximate date ranges that the kidnapper would need to have been in those cities. There were gaps, but I would bet that more than a few of those piles of ash had never been discovered, in who knows what cities, or—less likely—that some of the succubi who had disappeared had never been reported missing.

According to my list, the perp would have been in Phoenix before Chicago—kidnapping a succubus there. And prior to that, Anchorage, where a pile of ashes proving to be those of an unknown otherworlder was found near a police station.

I'd take it to Natalie, I decided. She hadn't called yet saying she'd found anything, but the information couldn't hurt for her to have. It might make her search quicker, and an obvious suspect might even become apparent. Hope surged within me and suddenly I was on my feet, full of energy, and barely able to stop myself from racing out the door.

I called Natalie's office as I walked to my car. No answer, but I figured she'd probably be in by the time I was able to drive there, so I headed for her office first. I drove with the radio blasting, focusing fully on the notes pounding in my brain to avoid thinking of anything else. But thoughts of Valerio Costa trickled in, forcing Bon Jovi's lyrics right out of my head. His crazy black salamander eyes—eyes that should have been creepy, but were somehow intensely sexy. The conviction in his voice when he insisted I was a good investigator. And the way his arms held me, so safely against him while I slept.

Oh boy.

I skidded around a turn, glaring at the car behind me

as they mashed their horn. No. I was not falling for Valerio Costa. I was not. The man had used me as bait. Even worse, he hadn't told me that was part of the plan. Why had he slept with me? Because he wanted to keep me in his room in case the kidnapper came looking for me? Maybe. Maybe not. Maybe I was just overreacting because of the stress of Elaine's kidnapping.

But what if I wasn't?

A great weight settled onto my chest, pushing the air from my lungs, the hope from my thoughts. So I drove fast, sang loud, and did everything I could to keep Valerio Costa out of my head and away from my heart.

Natalie Leigh's building was as pristine as always. The morning light reflected off the building's dark glass, and that bit of brightness imbued me with hope. I walked inside, lost in my thoughts, and ran into what felt like a brick wall. Cool hands on my arms steadied me, and I looked up and met the gaze of a familiar face and the strong scent of herbs swirled around me. It took me a moment to place the large man as the one I'd seen in the lobby when I'd visited Natalie alone about the burned body case. He dropped his hands and stared at me, as if his eyes would bore through me, sweat gathering on his forehead.

I stepped aside, uncomfortable. Did he work security for the building or something? A suit adorned his body, but he carried himself like professional muscle. He lugged a bag, and I wondered if that was where the herbal scent had come from. Perhaps he was a customer of Natalie's? Or a supplier?

I felt his eyes on my back, and I waved at the receptionist. Recognizing me, she nodded and reached for the phone. The witch, it seemed, wasn't one for surprises. I didn't look back, but headed for the elevator. Encouraging the man by acknowledging him was a bad idea.

Waiting patiently for the elevator to ding, I checked my cell phone. Still no call from Costa. No half-assed explanations. No attempts to get me to listen. No screw-yous. The fact that he hadn't even tried to call somehow made it worse. It hadn't been long, of course. Yet if he really cared, wouldn't he have followed me out of the hotel? But no. No chase. No call. No worries—for him, anyway. I grumbled and stuffed the phone back in my jacket as I boarded the elevator. I turned back and hit the button for Natalie's floor. The large man no longer watched me, and the revolving door still spun from his departure. One less thing to worry about.

I knew I should call Costa and give him a chance to explain. Tell him what I was taking to Natalie. That would be the mature thing to do. His partner was a bitch, but that didn't mean that he was as bad as her words made him appear. And I had a feeling that what he'd confided in me the night before wasn't a story he told carelessly, if he'd even shared it before. But as the light behind the numbers counted off the floors in the elevator, I couldn't force myself to take out my phone to make the call.

Natalie's office door stood ajar, but her office itself was empty. I frowned and rubbed my arms. Nothing appeared disturbed, no rustled papers or knocked-over chairs. Perhaps she just hadn't arrived for the day?

Her day planner sat on her desk, so I gave the office and waiting room a quick once-over and then flipped it open.

Today, she showed appointments starting at seven o'clock and going clear through eight tonight. For Natalie, appointments almost certainly meant she was in her casting room, which was situated down a hallway from her office. I'd seen it once, when we cast the locator spell to find Elaine. A spell we'd cast in vain.

I whistled under my breath. The rest of her upcoming week appeared just as full. When did she have time for a life? Or even to eat?

It was nine now, and her calendar listed an appointment from eight until ten. So where were they? Her note was in shorthand, but it looked like some sort of luck spell had been scheduled. A private client, then. The police department didn't believe in luck.

The door leading to the hallway between her office and spell room stood closed, and I considered for a moment going back there to see if she was busy casting. I grimaced. No. Probably not the smartest idea. Magic was tricky. I was no expert, but I was pretty certain that no one would be happy if I interrupted her spell. Who knew what the consequences could be? For all I knew, barging in there might make her blow us all up.

I glanced longingly at her computer, but jarring her mouse revealed the screen to be locked and that a password was needed. Just as well. How bad would it look if she walked in to find me on her computer? No way would she believe that I was just on there to Google some information while I waited. I suppressed a sigh and pulled out my phone. The screen was small and the speed wasn't up to what a real computer could do, but it would have to work.

I loaded the tiny browser and tapped my fingernails on

her desk while I waited for the search screen to load. When the box finally popped up, I typed in "Anchorage, Witch" and hit enter. It might be a long shot, but Anchorage was out of the way. It wasn't exactly a bustling city for visiting Covenant members. A high level member—or former member—might earn a spot in the paper if news was slow.

The search came up with hundreds of pages of results, and I scrolled through the first page without clicking on any of the links. Most were for local coven's websites. The second page netted very similar results, with the exception of one link.

The *Anchorage Daily News* listed an article about a bigwig witch visiting for some sort of new bill signing. I hit the link and waited impatiently for it to load. After what felt like forever, the page slowly came up, one inch at a time on the small screen, almost too small to read. I zoomed in on the page and checked the date. Four months ago. Yes. That fit the range all right. I scrolled down and then stopped abruptly.

No flipping way.

The name stood out to me on the screen as if bolded, as did his very small but very happy face on the included picture. Viktor Koslov. That put him in the right city during the right timeframe for two incidences: Anchorage and Chicago. And he was a powerful witch, powerful enough to have twisted a succubus's powers. Chicago might be a coincidence, but Anchorage, too?

As I stared at the picture, something else caught my attention. A large man stood in the background. The man I'd run into downstairs. My heart stopped.

Natalie.

If Koslov was involved in this, Natalie might not be safe. We'd had her looking into witches capable of pulling off the power transfer. I pushed up from the chair and strode toward the door to her casting room, but my hand froze on the knob. So what if Viktor had been in Alaska with the creepy man from the lobby? He might be one witch of many, especially if the legislation they passed was a big enough deal for him to go there to show his approval.

What if I was wrong, and I walked in there and someone got hurt?

I gritted my teeth and stepped away from the door. I pulled my phone out and hit the back button. Thankfully, the search screen loaded quickly, and with shaking fingers I typed in, "Koslov, Phoenix" on the small screen.

Time moved even more achingly slowly as I waited for the results to load. Finally, after what felt like hours, the first page of results appeared. As I took in the short summary of the first listing, my breath caught in my throat. Two months ago, Viktor Koslov had been in Phoenix. Perfect timing for when the succubus disappeared, and near the time a pile of ash had been found as well.

The evidence was circumstantial but convincing. Not only could Koslov have committed the crimes, he'd been in at least three cities at the right time to have done it. And according to Natalie, no witch would have been able to twist a succubus's power with the councilman in the same city without him knowing. The burned victims still didn't make sense unless…

An image of the professional muscle I'd seen downstairs flashed in my mind, and I rubbed my arms against a sudden chill. Could that man be the key? His grip had been cool, like Costa's. Was the professional muscle a salamander?

He'd smelled of herbs. Had Viktor sent him back for something? Natalie had to have rare, difficult-to-find herbs in her spell room. Maybe she'd had something Viktor wanted badly enough to send his man back for them. Or even more likely, he'd come back to make sure the scene was cleaned of anything that could be linked to Viktor.

I grabbed the knob and twisted, yanking open the door to the hallway that led to her casting room. Risks be damned. Natalie had to know as soon as possible that Viktor Koslov—one of the most powerful witches in the country, if not the world—was our kidnapper. Our killer.

Chapter Twelve

Deafening silence hit me; the only noise touching my ears was my own frantic footsteps. I made my way down the hall to the casting room and, feeling awkward, knocked. The noise echoed in the hallway, but no sounds answered it. I knocked once more before tentatively opening the door. I stepped back, but no lightning or fire or ice flew from the room to strike me. The room was dark.

"Hello? Natalie? It's Detective Whitman." I felt along the inside of the wall, fumbling until my fingertips touched a light switch. I flipped it on, then took in the room before me.

Spell ingredients littered the ground—herbs intermingled with pieces of glass and wire. Scorches touched the walls and bookcases. Her circle, which had been etched into the concrete floor as well as painted, didn't look right. I stared at it for a moment before I realized that the paint had been smudged, nearly removed from a one-foot section. Deep scratches trailed across the etching.

What the hell had happened? Burn marks—maybe from the salamander? The scratches could have been from a dodged spell. A lethal one by the looks of the scraped floor. Maybe Natalie fought them and lost. I looked over the room one last time before deciding that I wasn't knowledgeable enough about witchcraft to figure out exactly what had happened, and then I headed back to her office.

Had she been taken? The room looked like it had been through a battle, and I was pretty certain that two witches fighting would probably create a mess at least that big. I flipped back a page in her planner and my stomach dropped. Last night, penciled in for seven thirty, was the name Viktor.

I plucked her phone from the cradle and looked at the screen. The fancy output had several sorts of lists, including who she'd called, calls she'd missed, and incoming calls she'd actually answered. I thumbed through the list of outgoing calls for yesterday. Several before seven thirty. I tried the first. A woman answered with an informal, "Hello?" I muttered a, "Sorry, wrong number," and hung up the phone. The next number was to a deli down the street—probably her lunch or dinner order. I got lucky on number three.

La Maison.

One of the nicest hotels in the area, it was undoubtedly where Koslov stayed while he was in town. The building was also adjacent to the alley where we'd found the burned remains.

"Viktor Koslov's room," I said to the operator.

"One moment, please." The phone clicked and started ringing through, and I slammed the phone back on the cradle.

This was all my fault. I glanced at Natalie's picture, propped on her desk. She smiled from the arms of an older woman. My stomach sank. I had to help her. And fast. I itched to call Costa, to tell him what was going on and get his opinion on where we should go from here, but I couldn't do that. It wasn't proper procedure, for one. I had to call this in to my boss. For another, I didn't trust Costa. Oh sure, I knew enough about him to know he wasn't a criminal, but that didn't make him trustworthy when it came down to it. I'd only known the man for a few days, and his partner's words still reverberated through my mind.

I picked up the phone to call the station. Vasquez was going to love this.

The lieutenant didn't sound happy to hear my news, but after the third time I went through all of the evidence—the dates, the M.O., the mess in Natalie's casting room—he conceded that I might be on to something.

"All right. But this had better be airtight, Whitman. He's a goddamn Covenant council member. Are you still at the witch's office?" Vasquez sounded irritated, but not angry. That was good. He might actually believe me.

"I'm at Natalie's, but I'll head over to La Maison." I tapped Natalie's pen against her desk and wished that I had called from my cell phone. At least I'd be more mobile than I was calling from Natalie's landline.

"The hell you will," Vasquez grated. "You're to stay as far away from that hotel as possible. You're too close to this case, and I don't need any fuckups in the takedown."

"This is my sister, Vasquez!"

"I know that." He lowered his voice. "I'm not saying you haven't done some damn good investigating here, Whitman. You've gotten us enough to pick him up and search his room, at least. But you can't be there." He cleared his throat. "I'm sorry." And with that jaw-dropping announcement hanging in the air, he muttered, "I'll be in touch," and hung up the phone.

I gaped at the phone and tried to move past Vasquez's apology—something akin to a meteor hitting a house in its rarity—to try to plan my next move. I couldn't go to La Maison. Ignoring Vasquez in this would almost certainly cost me my badge. And what if we didn't catch Koslov? Then I'd be completely shut out. No, I couldn't go there.

I frowned and considered what I knew of Koslov and this perp's M.O. Chances were very slim that Elaine or Natalie would actually be at the hotel. It was a nice place and while I was certain they gave their best customers a lot of latitude, two kidnapped women would not go unnoticed or unreported. No. He'd keep them somewhere no one would notice them. My money was still on a warehouse or other out of the way dump.

I took a file folder from my bag and then stared at the list that the vampire Magister had given us. Even with me, Costa, and the officers Vasquez had ordered to help, we'd only checked half of the warehouses on the list. I looked at the plotted map and frowned. None of the warehouses were near La Maison, per se. Most were clear across town. Only two dots stood out on the map that were anywhere near Koslov's hotel. He'd want to keep her close, right?

"Great," I muttered. It was a long shot, but what else could I do? Going to the hotel wasn't an option. I might as well check out the warehouse. I couldn't just sit and wait to hear back from Vasquez.

I locked Natalie's office door on my way out. It was an easy to open handle lock, but I didn't have a key for the door outside the waiting room, which could be secured with a sturdy deadbolt. Then I took the elevator down to the lobby and stopped at the reception desk. "When was the last time you saw Natalie Leigh?"

"Pardon?" she asked, raising an eyebrow at my tone.

I flashed my badge to remind her that I wasn't just a pretty face, and asked her again. "When?"

She shrugged. "No idea. A few days, I guess. I see her going to lunch occasionally, or out for appointments."

"Days?" I asked incredulously.

"She doesn't check in with me; I work for the whole building. She'll send her schedule down occasionally. E-mail me when she doesn't want walk-ins. But other than you cops she doesn't get a lot of unexpected traffic."

"All right. No one goes into Natalie Leigh's office," I told the woman. "No one except cops. Got it?"

Her eyes widened, and she nodded hurriedly. Back-up would arrive soon. It would have to do. I couldn't wait around for them, even if they weren't under orders from Vasquez to keep me there, which they probably were.

I headed for my car and hoped that Koslov was already being cuffed.

Of the two warehouses that were closest to La Maison, I decided the one by the lake was probably the most likely place. It was slightly farther from the hotel than the other building but was situated in a more industrial area. The other building looked like it might just be close enough to a nearby strip mall for noise to be overheard. Other than a few distant large plants and some storage units, the one I chose to check first was quite isolated.

I parked a block from the warehouse and examined my phone. I should call Costa. I knew that. But I'd be damned if it wasn't difficult. I considered calling Mac instead, but she'd almost definitely been pulled in for the arrest at the hotel. Besides, I didn't want to put her job in jeopardy. Astrid would be much the same. Calling anyone on the freak squad was a bad idea. The ones who would help me could endanger their careers by doing so. The rest—like Vasquez—would order me expressly not to do what I planned. My only hope of a career after this was not receiving that direct order. That left Costa.

And his freakishly stunning redheaded partner.

I ground my teeth and hit his number. Three rings and it went to voice mail.

"Flipping A," I muttered. Was Costa in on the hotel bust, too? I didn't think Vasquez would likely be willing to pull the OWEA agent in for the bust, but if he hadn't had a choice... Costa could have been at the station when I called. It would have been difficult to hide an operation like that from the OWEA agent if he'd been in the building at the time. For-getting to call him was one thing, something Vasquez might do. Lying to an OWEA agent's face was something else altogether.

Maybe he just didn't want to talk to me.

Swallowing around a lump in my throat, I redialed his number. This time it went straight to voice mail. I took a deep breath and said, "I'm checking a warehouse near La Maison. Not sure if Vasquez filled you in, but I think our guy might be keeping them here—Elaine and Natalie." I let out the breath in a big *whoosh*. If Vasquez hadn't explained everything to Costa, he was out of luck. I couldn't leave all the details on his voice mail. I didn't have the time or the patience. I left the address of the warehouse in a long rush and then hit end on my phone. At least someone would know where I was.

I left the car parked a couple of blocks from the warehouse, and then pulled a crowbar and flashlight from my trunk. Getting in and out quickly was more important than making a quick getaway—I hoped. I stood by a building next to the one owned by the Chevaliers and did my best to stay out of sight. I kept my gun in its holster and carried the crow bar in one hand and the flashlight in the other.

The warehouse was old, but not as old as the ones we'd looked at across town. The metal was rusting in places, but it didn't look ready to fall over any second. The only window I could see was in the front door, along the top. Enter through the back or the front? Finally I decided to make my way to the back. I strode around and approached from behind, careful to do my best to appear I belonged. Sneaking around would cause more suspicion if someone saw me. Then again, in this area, dressed as I was in my neat skirt suit and short heels, just the sight of me was likely to draw attention.

Mud squicked around my shoes as I made my way to the back door. An even bigger window than the one that graced the front door was built into it, paned by small pieces of wood forming smaller windows. But the room beyond was dark, so I was just going to have to take a chance.

I smashed the small piece of glass closest to the deadbolt

and then paused, listening. My heart thudded so loudly it was hard to make out anything else. So I stopped and breathed, trying to calm myself, trying to listen. Nothing. I removed what I could of the glass with the crowbar and then reached in and turned the lock. Then, very slowly, I turned the handle and pushed the door.

The room beyond was dark, and I turned on my flashlight to see beyond the small space illuminated by the open door. The cobwebs in the corners of the room suggested the place was vacant, and the layer of dust on an old desk in one corner supported the suggestion. My shoulders dropped. It had been a small chance, but I'd hoped.

I shook my head. Search this place or move on? Moving on to the next warehouse seemed like the best idea. Wasting time here wouldn't get me anything.

I stepped back, then reached for the door when something caught my eye. Dirt and grime covered the floor—mostly. A small trail of less-dirty spots went from the door through to the opening into the next room. It wasn't clean, and there was nothing so obvious as footprints, but less dust coated its surface that the ones around it.

I frowned and chewed on the inside of my lip. A caretaker could have walked through here. Perhaps one of the Chevaliers who routinely checked out the properties? Maybe. But maybe not.

I slid my hand over my gun and stepped back into the warehouse, making my way farther in as quietly as I could. My gun caught a bit in the holster, and I tugged to get it out. I struggled with my flashlight and the crowbar in my other hand, before finally finding a balance that allowed me to hold both, if a bit precariously.

The air was cool and faintly damp—tinged with other things. Scents that made me think of back alleys and bars. I stopped and peered around a corner, swinging my flashlight and gun as I moved. Nothing.

As I crept forward, careful to avoid rustling the papers that appeared haphazardly along the floor, a bit of light caught my attention. That couldn't be the outside, could it? It seemed too close to be some sort of break in the wall, too minute to be a small window.

My flashlight revealed a door. To creep or to fling? I frowned. If a Covenant witch and his bodyguard were behind that door, they'd hardly be impressed by the noise and sound of me hurling open the door and shouting "police" at them. No, sneakiness was best. Besides, if I were lucky at all, they were being arrested at La Maison as I crept through the dirty warehouse.

I opened the door slowly, wincing as it creaked. The light was on. Electricity ran in this warehouse. Excitement surged through me and I stepped into the room.

Movement across the room immediately caught my attention. My eyes met Viktor Koslov's, and I swung the gun around without preamble.

"Police!" I shouted, and then I cried out as I felt pain surge from my hand and shoot up my arm. My gun clanked to the floor and I risked a glance. Blisters grew and bubbled on the backside of my hand, and tears sprang to my eyes. The pain overwhelmed me as I took in the damage to my flesh.

Koslov smiled and nodded to my side. I followed his gaze, blinking through the tears. Tall and built like a linebacker, the man from the lobby stood, arm outstretched, with eyes as black as night.

Chapter Thirteen

Faced with the salamander ready to burn me, and the Covenant witch ready to do who knew what to me, I raised my hands, wincing as the skin stretched with the movement. The burn hadn't reached my palm but rather had only touched the outside of my hand, extending from the middle knuckle of my fingers to several inches of my arm above my wrist. So he couldn't burn just anything, or he would have burned my palm, I figured. Directionally based? Like a person standing with a hose, he could point it and shoot, but not otherwise direct the flow of power? I should have asked Costa.

"Keep your hands up, Ms. Whitman," Koslov ordered. He nodded to the salamander and the big man took a step toward me.

My foot slid back as if it had a mind of its own and that mind was set to get the heck out of there. As the salamander raised a hand toward me, I swallowed hard.

"Please don't worry, Detective. Leon is merely going

to search you. You will be quite unharmed, I promise. Of course, your continued health is dependent upon your co-operation." The council member flashed a smile at me, and I supposed he thought it a comforting expression. I suppressed a shudder at the creepiness.

The salamander tossed my flashlight and crowbar into a corner of the room and picked my gun up from the floor, tucking it into his belt. Then he searched me quickly and with a brisk efficiency and confidence. Former law enforcement?

This got better and better.

"I just want my sister," I said, then added, "and Natalie. You guys can go, get out of town. I never saw you here."

Koslov chuckled, but Leon maintained his expressionless demeanor. "Oh yes, Detective. I'm sure that you'll keep your word when we leave." Koslov's humor faded. "Who knows that you are here?"

I snorted. "Everyone, of course. I called for backup on my way in." I had, sort of. Although a quick call to Costa hardly equated with really calling in the cavalry. But Koslov had no way of knowing that.

"Lie." Koslov gave me a small smile. "Nice try, but I'm a witch, Detective. And not an idiot." His gaze traveled down my body, but there was no real desire on his face, no lust. He looked at me with the cold calculation of a car salesman checking out the trade-in. Finally, he pursed his lips and said, "Well you're not as...young as I would like. But you're definitely attractive enough. Isn't she, Leon?"

Leon grunted.

"The police background will certainly reduce your value. Unless..." He snapped his fingers and a smile of pure greed appeared on his face. "Oh yes. This will be just fine. I'm sure

I have some potential customers who would like to work out on you some lingering issues with law enforcement, Detective."

The corner of my lip rose into a snarl and I struggled to keep my cool. "Just give me the women. Do you really think I was too stupid to call in for backup before barging in here?"

He grinned. "Oh yes. I think you were just that stupid. That's the thing about you cops—especially otherworlders. Always with something to prove. You're all a bunch of wannabe cowboys."

Dammit. I was stupid. But Costa would come for me, wouldn't he? He'd check his voice mail and head here, especially once they figured out that Koslov wasn't at the hotel. I just had to delay them.

"Put her in a room by the other two," Koslov ordered. He turned to a small desk with a laptop sitting on top of it that was situated farther into the room. The desk stood out in sharp contrast—new and shiny in a room full of old, dirty things. Apparently Koslov didn't like the idea of working at one of the old, dirty desks stacked in the corner of the room.

"Why are you doing this?" I called. When all else failed, try to get them to discuss their glorious plans.

"Really, Detective?" He crossed his arms. "Trying to get a villainous monologue out of me is the best you can do?"

Crap. "Well, I'm curious."

"So sorry to disappoint you, but I'm hardly going to discuss my affairs with a *woman*—a succubus besides." He turned back to the desk and the salamander took a step toward me.

"I just don't understand why you're moving on from

succubi? Surely the market for sirens isn't as flush."

He stiffened, whether it was because I knew more than he'd expected me to, or because he was just getting irritated at my prattle, I wasn't sure. His salamander paused and glanced at Koslov.

"I mean, I get the succubi thing. Pet sex slave that you can drain, that's gotta be pretty damn appealing to a lot of scum-suckers. But sirens?" I shrugged. "I just don't see the point. I mean, when a siren's power is used, sure you can control a person for a brief period of time, but they always remember that they were controlled afterward. And using a siren's power is treated the same by the law as using a gun."

Koslov turned to me, expression dark. He'd nearly reached his desk. "I wouldn't expect you to understand, succubus." He named my species with such venom I start-ed, and I thought I saw Leon stiffen next to me. "In fact, I wouldn't expect much at all from you. Heaven forbid you have enough imagination to consider the benefits of being able to drain a siren of its powers. While you don't get the long-term power over a person that succubus powers pro-vide, you do get their unwavering obedience during the song and for a time after. The song can be used to eliminate any witnesses as well."

I mentally winced, and Leon shifted his weight beside me. That was true enough. If a criminal had no morals, they could use the siren's song to make a victim kill themselves in any number of ways before the effect faded. "Then why do you keep killing them?"

He shrugged, raising his hands up as he did. "Succubi were quite easy; it was merely a bend of their inherent powers. A reversal, if you will. But sirens are not built to transfer power…the results are unpredictable and irreversible." His smile returned. "But don't you worry your pretty head about it. I'll figure it out. And if a few bitches die in the process…" He shrugged and the smile that blossomed on his face made bile rise in my throat. Whatever other goals moved him, I'd bet my badge that Koslov's primary motivation was hurting his victims.

I snorted. "Doesn't seem likely. I hope you don't run out of succubi anytime soon. Maybe you'll have to move on to incubi—and they're still pretty tough to find. Hope you have some women in your buyer ranks. Or maybe incubi just don't move you in the same way?" I watched his face carefully as I spoke, and the slight snarl that arose at my question clinched it for me. Koslov had a serious issue with women.

It fit.

He kidnapped female-only species, and succubi and sirens were women who could control people with their powers. "So what woman pissed you off, Koslov? Let me guess, Mommy was a little controlling? She didn't hug you enough?" I lowered my voice, as if I had an intimate secret to share. "Or maybe she hugged you a little too much?"

He snarled something in Russian at me, and then said, "Get her the fuck out of here!" to Leon.

"Guess you're just not good enough to do anything other than bend nature, anyway," I called out, keeping my smug grin firmly affixed to my face, but inside my chest my heart beat wildly, and I felt like I might explode from the tension. "Besides. I'm guessing that your succubus power transfers are highly exaggerated."

"Oh, I don't think so." He smirked and sauntered toward Leon. Koslov reached up and touched the taller man's shoulder, then slid his hand down, caressing the salamander's arm. Leon shuddered, and a muscle in his jaw twitched. Then Koslov stepped away and headed back toward his desk. Leon reached out and grabbed my arm, his grip iron against my skin.

My mouth dropped open and the pieces in my mind fell into place. No wonder the burned bodies had been left in such precarious places. He was controlling the salamander using succubus thrall? Holy hell, I didn't even want to know the lengths he'd had to go to in order to establish that control. Succubi powers were inseparably linked to sex. Had he been abusing Leon in the same way he set up the succubi he sold to be abused? Was he sleeping with him? Or was it rape?

I swallowed hard against the bile rising in my throat and looked at the salamander. God, was that why he'd stared at me, so oddly intense? I should have seen it. Should have noticed that he was trying to tell me something. Should have picked up on Koslov's magic.

I shook my head slightly. That's why Koslov had seemed just a little more charismatic than normal when I met him in Natalie's office. He carried the unconscious powers of a succubus as well—a small amount, anyway. I should have picked up on that. But there was no point in berating myself about it now. I'd have all the time in the world to mentally scold myself after Elaine was safe. Right now I had to concentrate on freeing her.

Across the room, Koslov's grin widened as he watched my expression. He knew. He knew that I had figured out what he was doing, how he was controlling his pet salamander, and my horror amused him. Leon's grip loosened on my arm, and I wondered if he was merely waiting for orders or if he again struggled with Koslov's influence.

If Leon was already struggling against the witch's control enough to leave hints for the police to find, could I free him with my own ability? I couldn't reverse Koslov's thrall, but maybe with a touch of my own power, it would weaken the witch's hold just enough for Leon to break free. All I had to do was drink in some of his energy, and a small amount of thrall would naturally pass to him. I'd never used it that way, but I knew that it was possible. The closest I'd ever come was trying to make myself appear even more attractive to my prom date in high school. I'd kept his attention, all right. But it hadn't kept the jerk from dumping me two weeks later for another girl.

"Take her, Leon." Koslov made his way to the desk, and his voice had regained its coolness, its calm. His interest in me gone.

Leon released my arm and motioned for me to go ahead, down a hallway to the right of where I'd come in. I stiffened my spine and walked past him.

A loud crash sounded behind us, and I pivoted around just in time to see Leon do the same.

"Police," Costa shouted as he entered the room.

He'd decided on the dramatic entrance.

Hope surged until I saw Leon raise his hands. I didn't know how his power compared to Costa's, but I knew Costa could be burned. The OWEA agent's attention was firmly focused on Koslov, and he wouldn't even have a chance to defend himself against the other salamander.

I grabbed Leon's arm, but he ignored me. Desperately I reached for his energy and tried to pull, but failed. I could feel it, but I couldn't touch it. Of course I couldn't touch it.

Succubi powers were heavily connected to sex and, barring that, desire. Other strong emotions could trigger succubus powers as well, but none so reliably as lust.

Dammit.

Leon tried halfheartedly to buck me off while taking a couple of stumbling steps toward Costa. Koslov had a hand raised at Costa, and was speaking—spewing lies to get Costa to let his guard down, no doubt. But Costa was having none of it. He shouted at Koslov again to get on the ground.

Grabbing energy was tricky business, especially for a succubus who never used that side of her power. But I could do this; it was as natural for me as breathing. It had certainly felt natural last night, when I had to force myself *not* to take energy from Costa. My heart leaped into my throat.

Costa. That was it.

I blinked through the tears in my eyes and tried again, grabbing the salamander's body in a full hug. He grunted in surprise, but didn't move his focus from Costa. He knew who the real threat was, or perhaps he was under specific orders from Koslov to protect him first.

I held on tightly, pain throbbing its way from my hand up my arm, and tried to think of Costa. I pushed away the outside world where Costa shouted at Koslov and Leon tried to squirm away from me. I thought of our night together. Of how he made me feel. Of how Costa's power felt licking along my skin while he made love to me. All the while, I reached for Leon's power. After a few seconds, it clicked.

A flash of worry shot through me. Was Costa watching? Would my actions confirm to him that I was just another succubus looking for a fix? And most haunting of all, would siphoning power from Leon change me?

Leon's power jumped from his skin to caress mine, shoving all of my worries and fears away with its seductive power. I could feel it, just a small drain on him, but it was there. Spurred by my success, I kept Costa firmly in my mind and tried to open the flow even more. The power no longer caressed, it burned with a slow pleasant heat. Flowing from his skin to mine, it rode my veins, racing through them into my head in a rush of power so heady I barely kept my grip on the large man. I gasped as the energy started to pour into me, and the power combined with the magic and thoughts of Costa heated my blood and made me suddenly ache to be back in his arms.

Then it wasn't just Costa and me in my thoughts. Leon was there, too. A man I knew almost nothing about. His emotions flitted through me. Despair. Lust. Helplessness. Love.

Rage so fierce it shook me to my core.

Leon growled and yanked me off his back, tossing me into the room with Costa and Koslov. I landed hard on my side, and the air flew from my lungs. I struggled up to my knees and looked back at Leon. The salamander, as if the small gesture of tossing me had taken his strength, fell to one knee and his head dropped. He looked around, dazed.

My mind fogged, and thoughts—important thoughts— stayed just outside of my grasp. I looked around dumbly. Only seconds had passed since I'd jumped on Leon, but it felt like forever. Long enough to get caught up in the man's explosive emotions. Long enough to get to know Koslov's captive salamander just enough to hurt for him. Long enough to almost lose myself in a man I didn't even know.

Costa was shouting something at Koslov, but the witch ignored him and seemed to be muttering under his breath. A bit of a green plant peeked out from his tightly clasped fist, and I yelled, "He's doing a spell!" at Costa.

"Put it down, Koslov," Costa said, his voice loud but calm.

Koslov muttered a final word and tossed the herb at us, and then dove under the desk. Costa shot, but I couldn't tell if he connected with Koslov because the room was suddenly filled with black smoke that coiled and then sprang around the room like a living thing. Unnatural and dark.

I cursed under my breath. A smoke spell to cover his escape? Nice move, but there were only so many ways out of the room. I resisted the urge to cough and fought to see through the acrid magical air.

As my throat and mouth burned, I realized we weren't dealing with a simple smoke spell. Dammit. Poison. I struggled to keep my mouth closed, but my eyes burned and my stomach rolled. Darkness threatened to overtake me, but I couldn't leave, not with Costa trapped. The smoke cleared enough to make out impressions of the men in the room, but I couldn't seem to shout for Costa, warn him. My mouth and lungs weren't working right.

A shape moved next to me and I reached out, grasping at clothes. Koslov, it had to be. The shape struggled and cursed at me, but I clung to it, ignoring the pain as one of my nails felt like it ripped from my fingertip. My other hand still hurt so badly it was hard to hold on, but I held.

Until I saw the fire.

Chapter Fourteen

The flames moved up Koslov's body, still difficult to see even as the smoke spell began to fade. Because as it disappeared, it was replaced by smoke from the fire licking his body. It traveled fast—too fast to be natural. From his stomach, it moved down to his shoes and up to touch his face.

I scrambled away from the flames, and the burn on my hand throbbed, bile crawled up my throat, and even though the smoke was clearing, it curled up in my lungs. I had to find Elaine and Natalie. Had to get them out before the fire spread. I stumbled to the hallway and then glanced back to yell for Costa. I was able to make out Koslov in the darkened air. His screams cut through the smoke, so loud it was as if they came out of the throat of a banshee.

And Leon, arms outstretched toward Koslov, grimaced, even as he burned the man who'd taken away his free will. Tears trailed their way down his soot-stained face.

Suddenly Costa was there, arm around me, pulling me to

the hall that Leon had been dragging me toward. I swallowed the bile in my throat and looked away from the scene behind me. Elaine had to be back there. And given Leon's frame of mind, I wouldn't be surprised if he burned the whole damn building down around us. We had to find Elaine and Natalie before that happened and get them—and ourselves—out of the building.

The air cleared the farther down the hallway we got. Doors lined the walls. My lungs burned, but the farther we moved from the smoke, the more the spells' effects dissipated.

"Elaine," I croaked as loudly as I could. "Natalie?"

No muffled sounds greeted us—not that I could hear over the waning screams behind us. "Oh my god, Costa. What if they aren't here?"

"They are," he said. "They have to be. Koslov probably just has a spell up to dampen sound."

Costa kicked down the first door and I kicked at the next, wishing I'd had the presence of mind to grab my crowbar from the floor where Leon had tossed it. These doors stood between Elaine and me—maybe the very one I was trying desperately to break. I had to get it down.

The cries no longer sounded from down the hall, and I wasn't sure if I hoped that was because Koslov was no longer suffering or because of a sound dampening spell that draped the entire section of the hall we walked in, keeping the sounds within a certain distance of their origin.

The door I worked on finally gave, and I almost fell into the room, my knee screaming in protest as my foot hit the ground. Light from the hallway poured into the room, and I stared dumbly at Elaine.

Dark circles surrounded her eyes and she looked thinner

than she had a week before, but she stared at me—wide-eyed and tied to a chair. Alive. I called something to Costa, and after a few second he appeared with a pocketknife to cut Elaine free. She flung herself into my arms. Adrenaline rushed through my body, and I squeezed her tight.

Costa was there, pulling me again. Elaine clung to me as we moved, and I saw Natalie, looking slightly rumpled but otherwise unharmed, next to Costa. She rubbed her wrists where she'd no doubt been restrained as well. I followed them down what felt like a never-ending hallway, half carrying Elaine with me. Then there was light. Fresh air filled my aching lungs. And sirens wailed loudly.

I held Elaine and Costa held us both until a paramedic took her from my arms. I followed them, but then Elaine was surrounded, and I was forced to hover around the edge of the bodies questioning her. Then Astrid was there, giving me water and asking questions that I couldn't seem to pull my mind together well enough to answer. A paramedic asked me something, but talking hurt my smoke-burned throat, and all I could stutter out was a question about Elaine.

"What the fuck were you thinking?" Vasquez asked, and I blinked at him. I hadn't even seen him approach.

"I'm sorry," I said, my voice low and raspy. The water I'd forced down had helped—but it wasn't a miracle cure.

He grimaced at my voice. "We'll talk about this tomorrow. Don't think you're free and clear on this stunt."

I nodded, and immediately regretted the motion. I wasn't sure if the smoke inhalation or the use of my very rusty conscious succubus powers was responsible, but something had given me a heck of a headache. But I was alive, and I'd see as many doctors as they wanted to throw at me after I got Elaine set up in the hospital.

Vasquez stomped off, and I saw him corner Costa near the ambulance. They were moving Elaine inside the vehicle, so I pushed up from the police car I'd been sitting on and headed for my sister.

Someone tall blocked my path, and it took me a few beats to wrap my mind around the red hair, the pursed lips, and the striking features.

"I don't have time to talk to you, Agent," I rasped, putting as much bitchiness into my voice as I could.

Beatrice raised an eyebrow at that. "You have your sister now. I'd say you have nothing but time." My gaze flew back to Elaine. Yes. They were definitely loading her up to go to the hospital. I needed to get into that ambulance.

She spared a quick glance over her shoulder, and when she looked back at me her expression had softened. "Look, I just wanted to tell you that I was sorry. I acted like a real bitch at the hotel. You didn't deserve that, and neither did Val. I get...protective of him sometimes." A smile touched her face, taking her from merely gorgeous to breathtaking. "Okay, scratch that. I get downright jealous."

I couldn't deal with this right now. I couldn't think about Costa or his ridiculously attractive partner. "I need to get on that ambulance," I said simply, and then shouldered past her. I waved at the paramedic who held the door and he paused, understanding. I threw a quick glance over my shoulder before jumping into the ambulance. But Costa was no longer talking to Vasquez—the OWEA agent was gone.

Chapter Fifteen

I stared at my teacup and tried to make plans for the day. Nearly a week had passed since Costa and I had saved Elaine and Natalie from the warehouse fire. The questions started only minutes after we'd escaped from the building. Questions from the paramedics about Elaine. Questions from Lieutenant Vasquez about Koslov. Questions from OWEA agents about Costa. So many damn questions, and all I wanted was to go home.

But I'd heard nothing from Costa. I knew that he had to be up to his ears with his own questions and reports and who knew what else, but I didn't have to be happy about it. Luckily my burns were easily treated on an outpatient basis. I just had to be careful with the bandages for the first few days. And Koslov's spell had been short-lived. My lungs and throat were raw, but as long as I kept my voice down, it didn't bother me too much.

Movement in the entryway between the hall and kitchen

drew my attention. Elaine, arms crossed with a frown creasing her face, leaned against the doorframe. "Any word?" she said simply.

I shook my head. I'd told her what happened during her kidnapping—most of it, anyway.

"You should call him." Her voice was firm. Strong. Like she hadn't just been held against her will for several days. Of course, she couldn't hide the full impacts from me. I'd heard her screaming in her sleep. I'd woken her from the nightmares.

"You should be resting."

"I'm tired of resting. Why don't you just call him?"

"Because there's no point." I took a sip of my tea and turned my eyes back to the table.

"Mari, look at me."

I took a deep breath and met her eyes, the same clear blue I saw in the mirror every morning. "I'm here for *you*," I said firmly. "I don't have time or energy to worry about Costa. You are my priority."

Tears welled in her eyes, and I'd crossed the room to pull her into my arms before I realized I'd moved. She squirmed and pushed me away, stepping back so she could capture my gaze again.

"Stop this. You can't keep me any safer than you already do. And I refuse to live my life in fear again. I lost years of my life that way. Years, Mari. And I cost you years of your life, too."

I shook my head furiously, but she didn't stop talking.

"You deserve this, big sister. You deserve a chance to be happy. You deserve a man who will make you happy. And if there's one thing I learned from all of this, it's that life can end at any time. We both need to live to the fullest while we can."

I opened my mouth to argue, but the doorbell rang, startling me, and I sloshed some of my tea onto the table.

A smile flashed on Elaine's face. "I'll be upstairs," she said, and then she turned and hurried away.

"Did you call him?" I hissed after her. But she just waved over her shoulder at me and disappeared up the stairs.

I took a deep breath and opened the door. Costa's expression was serious, and I had to restrain myself from jumping into his arms the moment I saw him.

"I'm sorry I didn't call," he said, stepping into the house.

I looked away from him, suddenly fighting a lump in my throat. "It's fine," I finally managed.

"No, it's not, but I wasn't able to call anyone. The fire... They suspected me, at first until they questioned all the witnesses. And then enough time passed that it seemed like it would be better for me to just come here, talk to you in person." He closed the door and stepped closer to me.

"And Elaine called you," I muttered, feeling somehow betrayed. I'd known Costa had been implicated but hadn't realized they'd given him such a hard time. After all, they'd interviewed me and I'd told them about Leon. But considering what had happened, I wasn't surprised by their extra thoroughness.

"There was that, yes."

His expression was something I'd never seen on him. Unsure and hesitant. A little sad. Suddenly I wanted nothing more than to wipe that sadness from his face. But I couldn't. Not yet.

"Explain to me what the hell happened in your hotel

room." Flashes of Bea's face hit me, and the humiliation I'd felt that morning came back in a rush. I stepped back, needing room between us.

"Bea questioned why I'd be working with you on this. I told her it was because I wanted to keep you close in case the kidnapper went for you." He grimaced and shoved his hands in his pockets. "That was bullshit, of course. It wouldn't have made any sense for the bastard to come after you, a cop. There were plenty of easier succubi around who would have made more sense."

"But she believed you?"

"She knew I was full of shit." He snorted. "But she wasn't in town, so there wasn't much she could do until…"

I nodded. "Were—are you involved with her or something?"

"No!" he said, and he stepped forward and grasped my shoulders. Startled, I looked up and met his eyes. He dropped his hands to his sides, and stepped back. "I'm sorry. No. We're close. We've been partners for years, and we've been through some shit together. But it's not like that. Not for me, at least. She's like a sister to me. She's just protective."

I believed him. I wasn't sure if it was Beatrice's apology after the fire, or the desperation in his eyes that did it, but I knew he was telling the truth.

"I should have come after you. Explained. I'm sorry. I haven't exactly been trusting since everything that happened with my brother, and honestly I was scared that you'd just tell me to go to hell."

I sighed. "I should have let you explain. Running out like that…it wasn't exactly the mature thing to do."

Sadness crisscrossed his features, but hope was there, too—just under the surface. It broke my heart. I closed the distance between us and wrapped my arms around him, pulling him into a hug.

He stepped closer and buried his face in my hair, his arms so tight around me I squeaked. He loosened his hold and looked at me, then moved a bit of my hair from my face, tucking it behind my ear. I smiled at him, and the tension drained from his features and the muscles under my hands. It felt so good to be in his arms again.

"I missed you," he said.

"Me, too," I whispered. He lowered his mouth to mine and kissed me gently, and I pressed myself against him, my body suddenly soft and in great need. Only the knowledge that Elaine was probably listening to us upstairs allowed me to break our kiss. When I pulled back, his intense expression almost made me decide I didn't care what Elaine did or did not hear. But I gave him a small smile and stepped back.

"I'm sure you know, but Koslov didn't make it," he said, and I nodded, still unsure exactly how I felt about that.

"Leon?"

"They're saying he died in there, too. The whole warehouse went up, you know."

"You don't sound convinced."

"I'm not sure fire could kill a salamander, even at those temperatures. Well, not most salamanders anyway. The OWEA also interviewed some of Leon's family."

"And?"

"Apparently he and Koslov were in a relationship for nearly a year. It ended right around the time Koslov started his succubi experiments."

I shuddered. "So Koslov decided to siphon a succubus's power for himself, to get back at Leon." I knew it was true;

it fit Leon's mixture of emotions and the brief flashes of memory I'd gotten from him while thralling the salamander.

Costa didn't ask how I knew that, but worry creased his brow. "Seems like it. And from what we could gather from his staff, Koslov has been growing seriously unstable the last couple of years. Not that the man could have ever been totally right, being willing to do what he did, but it'd been starting to show."

"Maybe because he took the power? A power his mind and body weren't built to handle."

"Maybe." He paused. "How are you doing?"

I shrugged. "I'm okay."

"You drained some energy from Leon, didn't you?"

I stiffened and headed for the kitchen. Costa trailed behind me. "Yes, but not enough to make a lasting connection. I'll be fine." That wasn't entirely true; I could still feel a bit of Leon, and that would never go away. But the presence was small, and so unformed it wasn't worth mentioning. I knew it would fade—if not disappear—in time. "Want some tea?" I asked.

He gave me a disgusted look. "Coffee?"

I smiled. "I guess I could dust off the coffeemaker."

He sat down at the kitchen table while I looked for the old tin of coffee I knew I had somewhere. "How is Elaine?"

"She's better than I expected her to be." There. An old tin of coffee hid behind a bag of flour. I turned to face Costa and waved the coffee at him. "She's already talking about going back to class. I think she's handling this better than I am, to be honest."

"So there are no lingering magical effects?"

"Not that Natalie could find. She doesn't think Koslov

had long enough to complete the spells." I looked away from Costa's intense gaze and focused on my kitchen window. The sun was out, sparkling against the grass. The first sunny day I'd seen in a while. "I talked to Natalie about Koslov."

"What did she say?"

"Apparently he's always had a bit of an issue with women. Natalie said that no one realized how deeply disturbed he was. He took Natalie when she started looking into that list of potential suspects for us. Guess he got nervous."

I heard footsteps against the tile, and the next thing I knew, Costa stood next to me. "Where does this leave us, Mari?"

I turned to face him, and his expression was open, full of emotions I couldn't name, and something in my heart twisted. But I didn't know what to say. I cared about him — far too much considering our short time together and the mobile nature of his job — but there it was.

He leaned in, and murmured against my ear, "I'm falling in love with you, *bella*. I'm afraid I'll crash and burn without you."

I grinned. "Well, I certainly wouldn't want you to burn."

This time, when he kissed me, I had a hard time letting him go.

Acknowledgments

There are so many people I owe a thank-you for their help and encouragement with this project. I want to give a huge thanks to:

My family, for always being there for me, and for supporting my choice to try this writing thing. I love you all so much!

My husband, Sash, who accepts my crazy writing hours in stride, and has been willing to entertain himself virtually every evening and weekend for the last two years. Thank you for believing in me.

Regan Summers, who not only gives up precious vacation time to read the stories I send her at the last minute, but who also continues to inspire me with her wonderfully written stories and awe-inspiring work ethic. Your friendship and support have made this whole thing possible for me.

Joshua Roots, who offers sage advice when it comes to improving my stories, and who encourages me with his own tenacity and hilarious writing. Thank you, my friend.

The rest of the Cantina crew on Absolute Write, for always being funny and kind. You are my haven.

Barbara Rogan, and my workshop group, for helping me strengthen my writing and for being amazing during releases. You are all talented and awesome.

My editor, Kerry Vail, for being a marvelous editor and friend. You have been my biggest cheerleader and my rock, and you have helped me grow so much as a writer. More than that, you've been such a good friend. There are no words to express how much your support means to me.

The rest of the Entangled team, especially Heather Howland, for seeing potential in my stories and helping me develop and market them.

About the Author

Tiffany Allee currently lives in Phoenix, AZ, by way of Chicago and Denver, and is happily married to a secret romantic. She spends her days working in Corporate America while daydreaming about sexy heroes, butt-kicking heroines, and interesting ways to kill people—for her books, of course. Her nights are reserved for writing and bothering her husband and cats (according to them). Her passions include reading, chocolate, travel, wine, and family.

Find out more at: http://www.tiffanyallee.com/